BIG FLIES

Julie —
embrace the
mystery!

Keith Hirshland

ISBN: 1532719361
ISBN 13: 9781532719363
Library of Congress Control Number: 2016908707
CreateSpace Independent Publishing Platform
North Charleston, South Carolina

"Mile upon mile got no direction,
We're all playing the same game.
We're all looking for redemption,
Just afraid to say the name.

So caught up now in pretending
That what we're seeking is the truth.
I'm not looking for a happy ending,
All I'm looking for is you."

—*Pat Green*

Inspired by a creative imagination.
Oh, and actual events.

PROLOGUE

There are hundreds, if not thousands, of unsolved robberies on the books or in the cold case files of law enforcement agencies all over the world. Four of the most famous happened in the span of fifteen years.

The Hijacking of Northwest Orient Flight 305 (the D. B. Cooper case)
On November 24, 1971, a man flying under the name of Dan Cooper notified a flight attendant, in the skies between Portland and Seattle, that he was in possession of a bomb; he threatened to blow up the plane if he did not receive $200,000 (approximately $1.5 million in today's dollars), four parachutes, and safe passage to Mexico. His demands were met en route to Mexico, between Portland, Oregon, and Reno, Nevada. Cooper, along with his $200,000 ransom, jumped from the aircraft. In July, 2016, the FBI announced they closed the case, "unless someone comes forward with the parachutes or the money". It remains the only unsolved crime in U.S. aviation history.

The Tucker Cross
In the mid-1950s, a priceless twenty-four-karat gold cross, embedded with seven large, sparkling emeralds, was discovered by explorer Teddy Tucker amid the 1594 shipwreck of the San Pedro, a vessel headed from Cuba to Spain. A quarter-century later, while on display in a Bermuda museum, the cross was stolen, and a cheap replica was left in its place. No one knows who perpetrated

the crime, but investigators have long assumed that the cross was melted down and the emeralds were sold on the black market.

The Chicago First National Bank Robbery
In 1977, $1 million mysteriously vanish from a locked money cart inside a heavily guarded vault at the Chicago First National Bank. The cash and the thieves are still at large.

Mexico City's National Museum of Anthropology
One hundred and forty valuable Aztec and Mayan figurines were stolen from the Mexico City National Museum of Anthropology on Christmas Eve, while guards were presumably distracted from their duty because of the holiday. Protected by only a seven-foot fence and a security system that had been broken for years, the museum was particularly vulnerable and the artifacts inside immensely valuable, as the crooks knew. One of the figurines, an obsidian monkey, was said to be worth $20 million alone.

It is unfathomable to think that all of these crimes were committed by the same person or people. Or is it?

THESE DAYS

"It was a dark and stormy night." His lips mouthed the words with slightly more speed than the index fingers of each hand could tap them out on the Apple keyboard.

Leland David knew that the great American storyteller Elmore Leonard cautioned prospective writers to "never lead with the weather." He also knew that first line sounded like the hackneyed start to a dime-store novel, but it really was a dark and stormy night. The shitty part was it followed a dark and stormy day. The dog, a two-year-old Bernese mountain dog named Harriet Potter, seemed unfazed by each rumble of thunder but let out a whimper after the occasional crack of lightning. The would-be author remembered that it was an imaginary lightning bolt that helped give the pup her name. The all-too-real bolts, the thunder, and the whimpering on this dark and stormy night made it tough to concentrate. Leland knew concentration was paramount when attempting to write the "great American novel."

Bang! went the weather.

Whimper, answered the Berner.

"Crap," the struggling novelist chimed in as he held down the backspace key, eliminating the cliché letter by letter.

Ring went a fourth player. It wasn't the elements, the dog, or the author this time; it was the sound of his mobile phone from another room. There were two ways to reach it in the hundred-year-old house where Leland lived, and, as he did with most things in his life, he chose the path of least resistance. But even that route, out the study, through a bedroom, and down the front stairs to the library, took longer than whomever it was on the other end of the line was willing to wait. Leland got there too late. The screen displayed a picture of the dog, head hanging out of the window of his Jeep Wagoneer, tongue hanging out of her mouth, instead of a caller ID. That person had moved on, and the number left behind was unfamiliar. Leland headed back upstairs, through the kitchen and the laundry room this time, remembering to bring the phone along in case that person, or anyone else for that matter, tried again.

When he returned to the study, the dog was gone.

"Potter!" barked Leland, but when the pooch didn't reemerge, he shrugged his shoulders, sat down at his desk, and stared at the electronically generated blank sheet of paper on his computer. Then, for the umpteenth time, he started what he hoped when finished would be his first book.

"It was a dark and stormy night," he wrote again.

Two hours later the weather had calmed, a calmer dog had returned, and the phone had yet to ring again. Oh, and "it was a dark and stormy night" were still the only words on the page. Leland decided to get up, go downstairs, and pour himself a drink. It was gin these days, pricey and populated with all sorts of fancy botanicals. He had expensive taste and a habit of falling victim to good marketing. Dozens of brands of small-batch bourbons had entered and exited his system, and after coming to the realization that the amount spent on liquid that transformed him into a less congenial, far more cantankerous person, was too high a price to pay, they left his liquor cabinet too. Now, he spent only slightly less money on an equally impressive assortment of gins and found them to be a far less destructive force in his life. He grabbed a glass; dumped in some clean, clear ice cubes; and pulled the cork on a bottle of Ransom "Old Tom." After two of those and a few minutes of *SportsCenter*, Leland decided it was as good a time as any to go to bed. Teeth brushed, face washed, he lay there and listened as the century-old structure settled around him. The house serenaded him with a chorus of snaps, crackles, and pops. The cereal-bowl symphony to which Leland David slipped into a deep, dream-filled sleep.

He slept the sleep of someone without a care in the world, and in many respects, that's exactly what Leland was. The father Leland knew, Chester Daniel David, spent his time writing travel guides and restaurant reviews for places he'd never visited and establishments at which he'd never eaten. Funny thing was his tomes were wildly popular, both before and after he unexpectedly perished in a single-car crash. The police report, a copy of which Leland morbidly still kept, stated faulty tires as the culprit. Two had blown at exactly the same time, sending the car careening out of control, through a barrier railing, and over the side of a cliff. Ironically or coincidentally—like Alanis Morissette, Leland could never get that right—Chester had just months before given the tire company, on top of whose rubber he perished, "Five Stars of David" (his copyrighted ratings system that, not surprisingly, never reached the level of importance of, say, Michelin's stars or the American Automobile Association's As).

Literally, or maybe more correctly figuratively, adding insult to injury, Chester's wife and Leland's biological mother, Lucille, had passed away two years earlier to the day, after choking on a popcorn shrimp at a restaurant in Chicago that had earned a mere "Star and a Half of David." Leland would discover that his father panned the restaurant even though Chester had never darkened the place's door. But Leland never knew that the fatal choking incident prompted his dad to rewrite the review in a subsequent edition, inserting right off the top that the eatery featured "killer" appetizers, and bumping up the rating to a respectable "Three and a Half Stars of David."

All this meant that when Leland attended his second funeral in as many years, he arrived a very rich, albeit parentless, young man. A young man who, thanks to financial planners, custodians, and managers, never had to work another day in his life. So he went about his life *not* doing just that. Instead he took and tried every job he could, figuring he had to find one that fitted him like a glove. He even worked for a brief time in a factory that manufactured linings for gloves, but, as with most of the jobs he tried, he found it unsatisfactory. He couldn't put his finger on exactly why.

The realization that his now-deceased dad was not exactly who he claimed to be came one day while he was standing in the attic of his father's house (a house Leland still owned, unable to let it go regardless of the fact that selling it would have netted a tidy profit). Quite by accident he stumbled across hundreds, if not thousands, of *National Geographic, LIFE, Travel & Leisure*, and other magazines describing places all over the globe that would earn the coveted "Stars of David" in the pages of the well-read *CDD Guide to Travel and Dining, Volumes 1–48*. Leland could have been disgusted, embarrassed, or furious, but instead he found himself impressed. After reading several articles in many of the publications and remembering what his father had written about the exact same places, he realized that, despite being a fraud, his father wasn't a plagiarizer but a fantasizer who shared his travel fantasies with the rest of the world. Leland came to the conclusion then and there that some of those creative juices just had to flow inside him as well, and he decided what he would do with the rest of his life: he would write! More than two dozen months later, "It was a dark and stormy night" was still as far as he had gotten.

THOSE DAYS

It was Saturday, the day after Chester David's eighth birthday. The night before, his family had enjoyed the boy's favorite meal of beef stew and apple pie ala mode. The handful of years he remembered, his mother had always asked him what he wanted for his birthday meal, and this time around he went with her beef stew, the pie, and the ice cream. The dessert was store bought, but his mom made a mean beef stew. He also opened gifts. He had asked for a Lionel electric train set, a BB gun, and a microscope. When he tore into the wrapping paper, he found a shiny new Erector Set, some plastic army men, the microscope he had asked for, and a book—a Hardy Boys mystery titled *A Figure in Hiding*.

That night he orchestrated an epic living-room-floor battle between the new army men and some toy dinosaurs that he had gotten as a gift the year before, put the Erector Set and microscope aside for a more detailed examination, and went to bed with the book. *A Figure in Hiding* was his first experience with the Hardy Boys, even though Frank and Joe had been "solving mysteries" for decades. It was 212 pages, and that night he read it cover to cover. He thought the heroes, Frank and Joe, were OK, but he found himself fascinated by the bad guy, Nick Cardoza. Nick was a crook, and in this particular story, he robbed the local movie theater, ran off with the cashbox, then broke into the Hardy Boys' house, blowing open their father, Fenton's, safe.

Chester was also captivated by the "evil" Malcolm Izmir, who was the ring leader of the notorious Goggler Gang, a group of thieves (including Nick Cardoza) that pilfered cars, boats, jewels, and cash and then submitted to appearance-altering plastic surgery in an effort to get away. In the end they didn't get away; it *was* a Hardy Boys mystery, after all, and Frank and Joe cracked another case. Chester drifted off to sleep, after starting the book from the beginning again, thinking about how, if he were a member of Izmir's Goggler Gang, he would have gotten away with it.

THESE DAYS

Leland sat in an aisle seat aboard the A320 Airbus jet bound for, oddly enough at the moment, he couldn't remember. Much more troubling than the suddenly consigned-to-oblivion destination was the eerie feeling that he recognized every third or fourth person boarding the plane.

Leland traveled a lot. Sometimes he flew for business (after he had convinced himself he *had* business to attend to), other times because it was the most convenient way to get to where he wanted to go, and lately, more often than not, he flew simply because he liked it. He found airports to be the perfect places to people watch, and despite the occasional delay, caused by machines being machines or Mother Nature, he realized that if he arrived at the airport in plenty of time, the process turned out to be quite enjoyable.

Coming through the boarding door at the moment was a woman Leland was sure was the prim and proper person who occasionally served him soup at the coffee shop/bakery down the street from his house. She was followed, a few folks later, by a dead ringer for the guy who sold him his big-screen TV. Then things got weirder. Was that the former Victoria Secret model now married to the NFL quarterback just ahead of the aforementioned NFL quarterback? *Could be, I guess*, thought Leland. *Or not*, he thought again as four people later, his fifth-grade teacher, Mr. Coyle, pulled a carry-on bag onto the jet. After Mr. Coyle came his dead dad's best friend, Don Richards, Glenn Frey, the author Stuart Woods, and San Francisco Giants legend Willie Mays. Leland suddenly knew he was dreaming, closed his eyes, and screamed at the top of his lungs in an effort to wake himself up.

It worked, because as soon as he opened his eyes again, the flow of foot traffic going by seat 8C was the normal, everyday riffraff of the world's flying public. Now, Leland focused on first class, noticed three open seats within his field of vision, and got annoyed all over again. He had earned star-studded status on this particular airline and wondered why he hadn't received an upgrade, and then he saw Morgan Fairchild, dressed as a flight attendant, come out of the lavatory. *Still dreaming,* he thought as he closed his eyes again.

Seconds later he was still in his airplane seat but no longer on the aisle inside the aircraft. Instead he found himself at a cemetery, the cemetery where both his mother and father were buried, staring at the tombstones, his mother's first.

Lucille David. Loving Mother, Devoted Wife was chiseled into the granite. Leland's hand reached for the ground, and he pulled up a few blades of grass, and then he shifted his gaze to the grey slab bearing his father's name.

Chester David
human, kind

No dates, no other descriptors, nothing else.

"What the hell did that mean?" Leland asked the breeze, not remembering seeing those words on the tombstone during prior visits to the gravesite.

"Why the ruse?"

"Who were you?"

More questions unanswered.

"What are you trying to tell me?" he wondered aloud, thinking of all those magazines with their stories on the inside and Chester David's story on the outside.

"What am I missing, and who can help me find it?"

Suddenly he felt wide awake and found himself sitting bolt upright. The dog, lying on the floor next to the bed, opened one eye, lapped her nose and upper lip with a wet, pink tongue, and rolled onto her left side. Leland could barely remember what he had just been dreaming, but something tugged at the back of his subconscious and caused him to utter one word: "Dad." At the sound Potter stood up, moved toward the bed, and set her head on the mattress. Leland slid down so he could be face to face with his companion. Her tongue shot out, landing wetly on her master's cheek. He distractedly wiped the saliva off his face and spoke again.

"I think it's time for a road trip, girl."

That news motivated Harriet Potter to wag her tail.

THOSE DAYS

The first spitball hit Chester in the top part of his left ear. The second, fired with a bit more force, got him on the cheek. It landed with a splat and stuck for a second that felt like forever to the reddening skin of Chester David's face. The wet wad of paper slipped onto his desk, but a tiny trickle of Marty Moran's shiny, stinky spittle remained until Chester wiped it off with the cuff of his once-clean shirtsleeve. A sudden wave of nausea swept over the boy, and he might have vomited right then and there were it not for a more dominant emotion of rage that just as quickly came over him. Most of the students, including Chester, were trying to take a math test. Marty Moran was busy trying to cheat off the smartest kid in the class. The bully had been picking on the smaller, smarter, more vulnerable kid for months, thinking he was circling easy prey. Initially Chester had been, but he was getting fed up.

"Psssst." Moran sprayed more spit and made a noise a little louder than he should have. Mr. Graffam, the math teacher, stood at the blackboard, back to the class, writing out a problem for future discussion. He hadn't heard, or chose not to hear, the disturbance behind him. Several of Chester's classmates not only heard but also looked up from their test sheets to see what would happen next.

"David!" Moran hissed. "Hey, dork!" he added louder as Chester continued to ignore the interruption. "Move your arm." Another wet wad of paper smacked into the back of Chester's head, this one from a straw still in the mouth of one of Moran's band of bootlickers. Instead of giving in, Charles hunkered down, covering his exam like a mother hen settling over a not-yet-hatched egg.

"Mr. G!" A different voice filled the room. It was the class butt kisser and know-it-all, Margaret "Maggie" Klein, trying to get the teacher's attention by using the nickname he'd asked them to use at the beginning of the year.

"Mr. G! Mr. G!" she repeated. The figure at the front of the room calmly set the piece of chalk down on the silver catchall that ran the length of the green board. The white chunk joined several dusty erasers as well as other random-sized bits of chalk. He slowly turned to face the pigtail-coiffed child nuisance. Upon being noticed, Maggie sat rod straight in her wooden seat, extended, and then waved her right hand.

"Misssster G!" she said a fourth time.

"Miss Klein," Mr. Graffam said, rather slowly, in a voice that exuded dissatisfaction, exasperation and even a little distaste, "you now have my undivided attention. But aren't you supposed to be taking a test?" Chester, and just about every child in the class, knew the question was a rhetorical one. Maggie dropped her hand and lowered her eyes.

"I'm trying," she whined, "but Marty Moran is making it *impossible*!" She spoke the last word more emphatically than needed while turning and pointing to the desk at which the pathological cheater now slumped. The teacher's gaze followed the girl's petite, nail-chewed, index finger.

"Ahh, Mr. Moran," he said, "aren't *you* supposed to be taking a test?"

"I am *trying* too," the ruffian said, mimicking his accuser, "but this little doofus won't stop bugging me." Moran pointed a stubby right thumb Chester's way. Two of his sycophant stooges snorted subdued sniggers, and their leader couldn't contain a smile. Miss Maggie Klein adamantly shook her head back and forth while Chester David waited, with anticipation, not moving a muscle.

"Is that so?" Mr. G. again addressed Moran, walking between the desks and settling in front of the big, lazy troublemaker.

"Yeah, that's so," Moran answered, indignant, defying the teacher to prove him wrong, which, of course, he did. Mr. Graffam turned his head to look at his prized pupil and saw three things: a beet-red-faced boy, both angry and embarrassed; a nearly completed (and the teacher already knew, 100 percent correct) math test; and several drying spitballs scattered on and around the child's desk. Then he looked back at the tormentor. He quickly reached for and then held up, between his thumb and forefinger like a smelly sock, an unblemished test sheet, filled with typed questions but no written answers.

"I think you need to *try* harder." Mr. G. smiled at the same time the smirk left Moran's mug. "And I think the principal's office is the perfect place for you to do just that. Get up."

Moran obeyed and allowed Mr. G. to lead him to the classroom door at the front of the room. The teacher held the disrupter's arm just above the elbow with his left hand and opened the door with his right, and then turned back to his students.

"Get back to work."

Before they exited Moran turned too, but he only had eyes for Chester, who captured and held his adversary's "this is as mean as I can look" gaze. Chester knew full well this wouldn't be the end of it, but suddenly he no longer cared. He was tired of being pushed around by Marty Moran and others like him. He was going to do something about it; he just wasn't sure what just yet.

THESE DAYS

Leland had been behind the wheel of the Jeep Wagoneer for a little more than ninety minutes trying to make sense of the conflicting information bouncing around his brain. When Chester David left this earth, his son was sad, to be sure, but in no way was he consumed by grief—not even close. In fact, as Leland drove east on Interstate 80, he tried to remember if he ever shed a tear over his father's passing. He couldn't, so he decided to decide that he must have. His dad was a decent guy and a better than decent provider, but as Leland drove on, he couldn't shake the feeling that the man was somehow incomplete. As a kid he always felt like there was something missing or something extra or something wrong. He recalled an on-again, off-again fantasy he harbored that his pop was some kind of superhero, saving people or righting wrongs. In less frequent but more vivid, unsteady moments, the same man was instead some kind of super villain—the *reason* why people needed to be protected, the *cause* of the wrongs that needed righting. Sure, when his dad was not "away on business," they did things fathers and sons do together, like learn to drive, go to ball games, and talk about girls, grades, and jobs. But he always sensed the presence of a hole, or a hardship, somewhere nearby. Lurking. In all but the very least-steady times, the boy was pretty sure whatever he could sense but couldn't see wasn't coming or missing from his old man's heart. When push came to shove,

Leland convinced himself it didn't matter that he thought his pop was a little strange, a little distant. He loved him and he knew, despite all his faults, real or imagined, his dad loved him back.

When Chester died and Leland subsequently discovered his secret—a little matter of making millions of dollars by duping millions of people into believing he was a travel expert and a sapient food critic—Leland did not feel anger or betrayal. He didn't feel embarrassed or injured either. He guessed it was more of an understanding. His dad wasn't *missing* anything, he was instead *hiding* something, maybe everything. Now it seemed knowledge of the deception had morphed into some version of a revelation that produced a nagging question. He suddenly had something on which to hang his proverbial hat—curiosity.

THOSE DAYS

Some people are legends in their own time, and some folks are legendary in their own minds. Donald Thompson Richards was somewhere in between. His exploits had certainly become the stuff of legend around the Sierra Nevada. Especially in the geographical area that stretched around Truckee, California, North Lake Tahoe, Nevada, and down the mountain into the Truckee Meadows. Around "those parts" he was known simply as Snoshu.

Most tell the story this way: Richards wasn't born or raised in the area, but in a short time after his arrival, he had become a local. Gregarious and well liked, he, on more than one occasion, over more than one beer, described his childhood to people. He was big as a kid, and though he always knew he could use that to his advantage against the other kids, he rarely did. He mostly kept to himself as a child. He had a few friends—one good one. As an adult Richards was around and then not around. Folks would remember stretches of time, sometimes weeks, when no one could remember seeing his smiling face. But he always came back and picked up where he left off. Through liquid and laughter, the thoughts of his disappearances disappeared, and life returned to normal. Another thing they remembered but rarely remarked on was that nobody could name a full-time job he held or a business at which he regularly worked.

Despite that, Don Richards always had enough money to do pretty much whatever he liked.

He liked to ski, he liked to hike, and he loved to explore the mountainous terrain, knowing no matter which way he turned or which trail he took, he would always end up where he wanted to be. He also never had a problem getting back. When he wasn't not getting lost, he could usually be found at a local establishment called the Forty-Niner. But the man constantly ran afoul of the pub's owner because he paid a bit too little attention to his ever-growing bar tab, even though everybody, including the owner, knew he could settle it any time he wanted. It didn't help that he also paid a bit too much attention to the barkeep who just happened to be the owner's latest girlfriend. The back story to the story was that Richards and the owner were actually good buddies, but the circumstances of Richards's affections (drinking and the girl) as well as his animus (paying for the drinks and respecting his friend) were putting a strain on the friendship. One knew the other had a weakness for women, whisky, and a good wager. The other knew one was a slave to his emotions and an under estimator of talent and tenacity. A challenge was proposed, and stakes were agreed upon.

The storytellers had a ball with the next part: describing the test of wills. The owner of the Forty-Niner had dreamed up a combination of scavenger hunt, eco-challenge, and flat-out race around the seventy-two miles that made up Lake Tahoe's perimeter to get the nightmare that had become Don Richards out of his life. Richards accepted the challenge immediately. Surprised, and a little worried by that, the bar owner decided he'd make it even more difficult, adding to the physical challenge by putting a time limit on the endeavor. Since Richards had already so readily agreed to the initial terms, the owner knew that, regardless of the new restrictions, this test was too tempting for Richards to turn down. He was also positive it would be too prohibitive for the man to pull off. He would turn out to be right—then wrong.

A date was set, December 19, and the stakes were determined. If the owner ended up victorious, Richards would pay his bar tab in full, give up on the girl, and never darken the door of the Forty-Niner again. If, however, Richards happened to defy all odds and come out on top, his five-figure bar tab would not only be forgiven, but Richards would also find himself a 51 percent owner of the place in which he spent most of his time and too little of his money.

THESE DAYS

The stretch of road on which Leland now traveled was familiar and comforting. It was a highway that climbed from west to east into the Sierra Nevada mountain range. He pushed past Newcastle, then Gold Run and Dutch Flat, heading into the Tahoe National Forest with Blue Canyon sprawling out past the driver's side window. He knew next up would be the ski areas he visited as a kid: Royal Gorge, Sugar Bowl, Boreal Ridge, and Tahoe Donner. He was also well aware he would wind through the mountains until he reached historic and beautiful Donner Lake, named for the tragic group of pioneers who, while looking for a better life, wandered into this inhospitable terrain during an uncompromising winter and ended up finding nothing but despair and death. Leland knew the history of the Donner party and marveled at their courage. He was always well aware he would not have had what it took to not only forge a life in that day and age, but also set out with everything he owned in the bed of a wagon or on the back of a horse across an eight-thousand-foot-high mountain range to find and make a better one.

For the most part, Leland David was the type of guy who let life come and go around him. When he was a kid, he dreamt of playing professional baseball, but as an eleven-year-old, he faced a fireballing, slightly wild teenager named Dwight Agarn, who hit him square in the head with a curveball that failed to curve. The effect was a sudden, and seemingly never ending, predilection to bail out of the batter's box anytime any pitcher threw him anything resembling a breaking ball. Baseball career over.

He always liked music, the lyrics more than the melody, and once thought he could write that next *Billboard* chart topper. In what he himself could only describe as an overnight jolt of genius, he awakened one morning and penned the words to a ditty about a girlfriend-stealing lothario. He titled it "He's Got a Way with Women" and was most proud that the chorus included the very clever play on words, "and he just got away with mine." He included a chord progression, but before he packed up and moved to Nashville so artists could beat down his door, he played it on his guitar for his best friend, Dave Hilliard. His buddy listened to the entire song, then chuckled, said it was genius, and saved Leland from abject ridicule by informing him that Rodney Lay and Hank Thompson had beaten the wannabe Paul Simon to the punch by jotting down those very words in the 1960s. Songwriting career over.

A few years later, he thought inventing something was the way to go and started the process of filing patents for what he was sure were two "next big thing" ideas. The first was a "drool collector." He felt the idea was both ingenious and simple. It featured a tiny plastic bucket, slightly larger than the thimble game piece in Monopoly, attached to a plastic hook. Just before bed, or a nap, a person would hang the hook from the side of his or her mouth so when that person experienced the inconvenience of excess saliva while sleeping, the embarrassing drool would simply collect in the container instead of on the cheek, chin, or pillowcase.

The next can't-miss creation was inspired by his often-gone, always-traveling father. He figured no self-respecting businessperson traveling the world would want to suffer the indignity of having to call the front desk of a four-star hotel in the middle of the night because the commode was backing up. So he conjured up the "travel plunger" and sketched out the plans for a plastic and rubber folding tool, small enough to fit in a suitcase but large enough to tackle the biggest problems. Needless to say, neither idea bore fruit.

As he drove on, he came to the realization that he had spent his life asking relatively few questions because he never felt like he needed many answers. But that all changed overnight when a singular question bombarded into his subconscious and then wiggled its way into his conscious and grabbed hold—suddenly hoping, needing, begging, to be answered. The dog stood up in the back of the Jeep and stared at the driver through the rearview mirror. On cue Leland pulled over at the scenic lookout near Donner Summit and let the pup out to pee. He watched her do her business and thought back to the day she came into his life.

THOSE DAYS

Like Marty Moran, Chester David met Don Richards in school. The first time they became aware of one another was in an alley that linked their mutual place of learning and a mom-and-pop convenience store that sold candy and soda to kids on their way to and home from classes.

Richards stumbled upon Chester, who was about to get the crap beaten out of him by a bully, clearly pissed that Chester hadn't agreed to share the answers to a quiz. Richards didn't know Chester very well, so he neither liked nor disliked the geeky kid, but he did know Moran, and he didn't like the bully. Before the first, and probably only, blow could be delivered, the newcomer inserted himself into the situation by walking up and standing right behind the prospective punching bag. That simple act was more than enough to convince the simpleton that he wanted no part of a real opponent, so he bolted.

"I can take care of myself," a shaking, fist-still-clenched Chester David muttered just loud enough for the burlier boy-turned-unsuspecting-bodyguard to hear.

"Never said you couldn't," Richards replied, and turned to walk down the alley.

Catching up, Chester added, "I had it under control." He stuffed his hands in his pockets and looked at his shoe tops.

"Yep, completely." His unlikely protector walked, head held high, straight ahead. The tone, more than the words, struck Chester like the punch he had moments ago expected from the school bully. He stopped, so did Richards, giving Chester a chance to get a good look at his companion. What he saw was a good-looking, muscular kid standing at least a head taller than him, who smiled, pulled his huge hands out of his jeans pockets, and shrugged. The boy and the gesture made Chester feel smaller, less handsome, and in a strange way, more defiant.

"I've been reading about martial arts and boxing techniques," he blurted, hoping to achieve some semblance of self-respect from the situation.

"Good to know," Richards shot back, dismissing Chester in three monosyllabic words. He paused, looked at the sky, and then back, meeting his alley mate eye to eye.

"Look, kid—"

"Chester."

"Look, Chet," Richards said, continuing.

"Chester," Chester repeated.

Richards sighed. "Look, *Chester,* I wasn't trying to butt in on your fight. I wasn't there to be your bodyguard. I just happened to be in the wrong place at the wrong time."

Chester looked again at his shoe tops and then back up. "More like the right place and the right time for me." He smiled.

Richards laughed out loud. "Is that a thank-you?" he asked, slapping Chester on the back.

The kid stood stock-still and continued to smile. Suddenly Richards realized he wasn't looking at a wimp, just a kid, and a decent-looking one at that. He noticed *Chester* had sharper features than the ones he saw when he looked at himself in the mirror, along with bright-blue eyes, a thick head of hair, and straight, white teeth. He thought it would have been a shame to see any of it blackened, pulled, or knocked out in the alley. Just as suddenly he realized he was actually happy he had happened upon the beating before it had a chance to take place.

At the same time, Chester continued to size up his protector. He couldn't help but notice Richards had short dark hair, unsmiling brown eyes, and a softer, wider nose than his own. *Was that the early stages of a moustache on his upper lip?* Chester thought enviously.

"Why did those punks want to rough you up?" the almost moustache asked, bringing Chester back to the moment.

"Wasn't *those* punks," he practically spat, "just *one* punk."

"Moran the moron," Richards said, shaking his head. "What's his beef?"

"This time?" The smile disappeared for a second. "I wouldn't let him cheat off my math quiz," Chester said, and started to smile again.

Richards knew of Marty Moran's reputation as both a bully and a dummy. He also knew Chester's rep as the smartest kid in class, maybe the entire school. After getting a good look at the kid, he no longer saw the stereotypically nerdy wuss, just a regular kid, albeit a super smart, smaller-than-average one. He also couldn't help but notice the fairly large chip on Chester's shoulder. It was hard to miss. They had reached Lander's, the mom-and-pop convenience store that catered to, among other folks, kids after school.

"Going in?" Chester off-handedly asked.

"Might. You?"

"Yep. Always get a pack of baseball cards and some red licorice."

"I get cards too," the taller boy said, perhaps a bit more enthusiastically than he had intended, "and sometimes a chocolate ice-cream malt."

"Never tried one of those," Chester said, opening the door and holding it for Richards.

"You got to," he said, walking inside.

Chester David didn't have any friends, and Donald Richards seemed to have plenty, so he probably wasn't looking for more. But suddenly a friendship was born from a chance breakup of an impending beatdown.

THESE DAYS

S omebody, somewhere, either in person or on a television show, suggested that getting a dog was a great way for single guys to meet single girls. Leland had the time, the interest, and the money to get a puppy, and conveniently, for the reasons espoused, he was girlfriend-less at the time, so he figured, why not? With the type of pet picked, he next concentrated on the breed. He knew he wanted a big dog, not Great Dane big, but big, so he did some research. He looked at websites, books, and magazines and became very interested in the look and most everything he read about the Bernese mountain dog. The next step was to find and meet a reputable breeder who would, in turn, find Leland a worthy owner. He filled out questionnaires, spoke to people on the phone, and finally made a connection that ended up being a perfect match. It all added up to Leland David being put on a waiting list for a puppy. The entire process held his interest and gave him something to do, and he always welcomed something, with a purpose, to do. The breeder accepted Leland as a client, then asked for a hefty, nonrefundable deposit, and announced that he would let the future owner know when the "AKC champion and multiple-award winning bitch" had her litter.

Seven puppies popped out. During one of the early conversations, the breeder informed Leland that the four "best" were already spoken for by people who either wanted to show or breed the dogs themselves, but Leland would be first in line to choose one of the rest. He was allowed to visit for the first time when the puppies were five weeks old, so on that day he hopped in the Jeep, drove about ninety miles, and fell in with a passel of little pooches. He sat on the floor in the middle of a large room surrounded by eager little mouths and wagging, tiny tails. He tried to make it a point to play with all seven pups, and he was successful with six. They tugged at his pants legs and nipped at his fingers, but one couldn't be bothered. It was a female and appeared to be the runt of the litter. The breeder called her "pink girl" because she wore a pink collar as a distinguisher, but that wasn't the only thing that set her apart. She was alternately interested in a ball, then a blanket, then a rope toy. Basically she found anything and everything more to her liking than the goofy human in the center of the floor. Her siblings included three boys (yellow, green, and blue collars) along with three other girls (red, orange, and purple collars). They were black, white, and tan all over, and all over him. But not her, not once. Leland left that day determined to win her over.

He spent the first few minutes of the next visit in the same place, exhibiting the same posture as before, and the results were the same too. Six slightly bigger puppies, with slightly sharper teeth, used him as their personal playground, but "pink girl" was still just as content to play at her own pace, with her own toys. Unfazed, Leland pulled one puppy off his head, slid another off his lap, and crab walked over to the apathetic little animal. She grudgingly acknowledged his presence with a barely perceptible look and continued to chew on one end of a rainbow-colored rope toy. He adjusted his position so he was lying flat on his stomach, face-to-face with the cutest face he'd ever seen. He took the other end of the toy in his hand and gave it a little tug. Pink girl tugged back.

"You want to play?"

She dropped the toy, yawned, and wandered a few steps away before finding a place on one of the white pads scattered around the room to pee. Disappointed but undaunted, Leland figured two could play that game, so he turned his attention back to the pile of six pups. Seconds later he felt a bump on his lower back. He looked over his shoulder, and his heart melted. There was the puppy he wanted most, rainbow rope toy in her mouth, back for more. He spun her way and tugged again at his end of the toy. Instead of tugging back, she let loose of the rope and bounded up on his lap. Pink girl licked his fingers, and when he picked her up, she did the same thing to his nose. Then they were both bombarded by legs and teeth and paws and tails.

THOSE DAYS

Don Richards stood in front of Emmett and Evelyn Lander's house and thought about all the times he had been there with his friend, Chester David. He remembered the first visit to the home attached to the convenience store. He recalled the last time too, and all the times in between, but this was the first time he made this trip alone. He had to admit he liked Chester from the get-go; then he grew to respect him and finally admire him. He also learned more than a thing or two along the way. Chester was book-smart. Their mentor, Emmett Lander, was street-smart. He was pretty sure he knew what both thought of him, but he liked to think he was a little of both. One of the things Richards admired most about both the old and the young man was their ability to get everybody aligned in support of the job. Big or small, whatever the cause. *What* they were doing rarely mattered. The *why* seemed evident, but Richards wanted to learn as much as he could about the *how*. So he went to the source.

He had second thoughts before coming and had them again standing near the front door. After a couple of deep breaths, he decided maybe this solo visit could wait for another time, a different day. He suddenly pivoted on his right foot and spun halfway around, ready to return the way he had come. Inside the house, Lander watched through the peephole in the door and nodded in satisfaction when Richards, just as swiftly, completed the 360-degree turn and faced the front door again. *Atta boy,* thought the old man as Richards retreated into the house to wait. He didn't have to wait long.

Don had never been alone with Lander, and it showed. His nerves manifested themselves in the uncomfortable form of wide, wet eyes and a desert-dry mouth. When he opened that mouth up to speak, no words came out—just a couple of primal grunts and an awkward reptilian croak. Panicked, he tried to swallow, but without saliva that was impossible.

"Relax, son." Lander pushed forward his own half-drunk glass of water. "Grab a good gulp, and tell me why we're here." Richards did both.

When he finished, he took another swig and set the glass back on the coaster. Lander laughed out loud and then regarded his young charge in a far more complimentary light. Without a word, and before Richards could expound on his quest for knowledge by asking another question, Lander pulled a book from one of his library shelves and set it in front of the still wide-eyed but far more comfortable student. Richards immediately noticed the cover, which featured a lot of words in smaller print and two words in big, bold letters: **COGNITIVE PSYCHOLOGY**. It looked a lot like one of the textbooks Richards was usually loathe to crack open, but Lander opened it for him and flipped the pages until he settled on a section called *Psychological Priming.* Then he left the room.

Richards read and soon realized that while it may have looked like a schoolbook, it read like a page-turner. The words painted a fascinating picture of the theory behind a technique that could help one person get what he wanted from another simply by suggesting or planting words and ideas in his or her mind. Those words, according to the book, told with enough regularity, could, and many times would, affect decisions that might be made at a later date. Richards took the text and the theory to heart and practiced the tricks whenever he could, especially at home. Even though he wasn't, he'd mention studying the Irish potato famine every day after school and wasn't surprised to find baked potatoes on the dinner table for the first time in months. He overheard his parents say he was getting a new pair of skis for Christmas and used the time between the discovery and the actual day using a word associated with the particular brand of ski he wanted in as many ways as possible. He woke up Christmas morning thrilled, but not shocked, to find a shiny new pair of Heads under the tree.

He became convinced psychological priming worked on his parents, helped persuade most of his friends (Chester being the exception), and once or twice swayed a teacher or two. With all that success, when the time came, he harbored no doubt that he could manipulate the mind of an occasionally drunk, overemotional friend who happened to own a bar. Maybe it was that he wanted to prove to both his friend and his mentor that he was just as clever, if not as smart, as the two of them. Or maybe he just needed to prove that to himself. He wanted to show that his contributions to the team were worthy. What he failed to grasp completely was that his partners knew how much he brought to the table long before he did.

So Don Richards set his sights on his prey. At the 19th hole after golf matches, Richards made sure the Forty-Niner owner won, and he would publicly proclaim his desire to give it all up and pan for gold. In the next breath, he would question his competency when it came to completing a wintertime foot race around the seventy-two-mile perimeter of Lake Tahoe, especially in a specified amount of time. Over and over again, sometimes during a meal of a burger and a beer, he discussed his disdain for Studebaker cars, specifically the 1947 Champion model. Whenever asked, and even when not, he would opine that *Huckleberry Finn* was a great Twain read, but sadly *Tom Sawyer* didn't pass muster. And more than once, sometimes after a good movie, he worried aloud about being attacked by a bull moose "with those huge antlers" on nights that he had to wobble home from the bar. As a result of what he had learned—and learned how to put to good use—Don Richards not only could predict that there would be a physical challenge in his future, but he was also able to map out his route and stockpile several interesting items in his garage. He *knew* one day it would all come in handy.

THESE DAYS

Bernese mountain dogs have a white stripe of fur that runs from the top of their heads, right between the eyes, and down to and around what starts out as a pink, but in months becomes an all-black, nose. Pink girl's markings were less uniform than many of her siblings and reminded Leland of something right off the bat. Instead of being straight, the pup's white stripe was straight out of central casting for the canine version of the best-selling book, *Harry Potter and the Sorcerer's Stone*. The not-so-straight stripe actually looked like the doggie version of Voldemort having blasted her right between the eyes, creating a white lightning bolt of fur and making her the chosen one. In Leland's eyes that's exactly what she was.

White Lightning was one name that popped into his head for the pup, only to be dismissed seconds later when it conjured up images of an overacting John Travolta singing a song in the movie *Grease*. He also thought, chuckling to himself, that Bunsen would be a great name for a Berner but dismissed that too when he decided he couldn't, with a clear conscience, saddle an innocent, adorable, unsuspecting puppy with such a corny name that, in the end, might only be amusing to him. In subsequent days he mulled over more names and made two more visits before finally picking up the eight-week-old, newest member of the David family. By then he had made up his mind that pink girl's name would be Harriet Potter. Over the first year of her life, Harriet's marking mellowed and the white stripe on her forehead became more uniform, but the magic spell the dog cast on Leland that very first day only grew stronger.

As he ushered the relieved dog back in the Jeep, he thought about why he got her in the first place: to meet girls. To be fair he *had* actually run across plenty of members of the opposite sex with the dog. But he never met one whom he liked enough or wanted to work hard enough to make her like him enough. He actually came to realize he usually ended up remembering the dog's names, but not the owner's and that was OK by him. Leland David had been told more than once by more than one person that he was a good-looking guy, but he didn't see it so clearly when he looked in the mirror. He was tall enough, six foot two, and had fairly straight, white teeth; clear-blue eyes; and a head full of brownish-black hair. It was currently cut short but through the years had seen a ponytail, a perm, and a mullet. He had always been blessed with a clear complexion. In fact, in high school, while his classmates and buddies battled pimples, Leland never once had to buy a tube of Oxy cream. Of course he had a pimple or two here and there, but only here and there. He had a straight chin; a Roman nose; and average, unremarkable ears. He had girlfriends, good friends, and best friends growing up, but as decades passed and the distance between boyhood and manhood lengthened, the friends of the past became memories in the present. Leland, in general, wasn't a hard worker, and that included relationships.

Harriet Potter became simply Potter, and in those early days, it was easy for everyone who had read the book and met the puppy to make the connection thanks to the lightning bolt of white fur between her eyes. But when the puppy grew and changed and became a beautiful ninety-pound dog with a rather regular white stripe down her forehead, Leland started getting quizzical looks when he said her name was Potter. For a time, he tried to explain how the girl got her name but eventually grew weary of that exercise and decided it would be a closely held secret between himself and the dog. For the record, the dog agreed. He shifted his weight behind the wheel and continued his journey along Interstate 80 toward Lake Tahoe and the search for an answer to his suddenly burning "Daddy issue."

He had discovered his father was a charlatan, and he had come to accept that, but what had awakened him that night and nagged at him to this day was this: His father clearly never went to any of the places about which he wrote, but Leland realized his dad was never home either. So now he needed to know where in the hell Chester David actually did go when he went away. And what business was he up to when everyone thought he was away on business. Someone besides his now-dead dad had to have the answers, and Leland had an idea who that might be. Now all he had to do was find him.

THOSE DAYS

The middle of December can be brutally cold in the Sierra Nevada, and it seemed to get more and more inclement each time "the tale of Snoshu Richards and the Forty-Niner bar bet" was told. No matter how many revisions were made to the way the story started or the particulars embellished, it always ended like this: The owner of the saloon was enjoying a premature celebratory shot of tequila when, a full six hours, fourteen minutes, and thirty-seven seconds before the agreed upon deadline, Don Richards burst through the double swinging doors. He had managed to not only come up with every item on the scavenger-hunt list (which somehow included, but was not limited to, a bull moose antler, a prospector's pan, a paperback copy of Mark Twain's *Tom Sawyer*, and a hubcap from a 1947 Studebaker Champion), but also had in his possession a bottle of Old Van Winkle pre-Prohibition bourbon, a beautiful brunette on each arm, and a pair of handwoven snowshoes strapped to his back. The proprietor bellowed with rage and swore up and down that there was no way Richards could have come by his success honestly. Don Richards ignored the accusations and simply set his booty at the feet of the loser, checked each item off the list, and then flamboyantly checked his watch to reaffirm he still had time on the clock. As a consolation prize, he offered his friend a sip of the premium whisky but was rebuffed with another rant decrying the authenticity of many of the items and demanding a professional audit.

This back-and-forth went on for hours as the friends of Snoshu and the friends of "Snoshu's friend" hurled insults through the cigar smoke, alcohol haze, and flatulence—each side becoming more and more inebriated and ultimately more and more enamored with the roguish Richards. Finally, long after closing time, the bourbon was gone and so was the fight out of the now former majority owner. Toasts were made and "hip, hip, hoorays" were hollered as the racketeer and his mark hugged it out. From that moment on, Don Richards owned most of his favorite bar *and* a nickname. In reality he had no interest in owning the establishment but was extremely interested in owning and cultivating the nickname. So his first decree was to bestow the title of general manager in charge of day-to-day operations upon the previous owner. Then he gave the new GM a healthy raise. His next move was to fire the bartender and immediately ask her to be his wife. The new GM said yes, the old bartender said no thanks, the brunettes kissed Richards on each cheek, and everybody raised another glass of whatever they were drinking. "To Snoshu!" they shouted.

To Snoshu, Richards repeated silently.

With the scavenger-hunt items nailed to various walls like museum pieces and the tale told all around the western states, business at the bar boomed. Despite all of that success, the old owner, when drunk, continued to tell anyone who would listen that he knew Snoshu had cheated and how he was bound and determined to prove it. Eventually, people stopped listening, and Don Richards continued to do what he did from day one—not care.

THESE DAYS

Leland drove past the Northstar Resort and remembered that when he was a kid, it didn't even exist. This stretch of pavement would take him parallel to the Truckee River and through the Ponderosa Pines straight up and then down the mountain to a traffic light *T* at North Lake Boulevard. As he slowed to a stop, he knew going right kept him in California, going left led him into Nevada, and going straight would get him nowhere except through a business or two and into world-famous Lake Tahoe. Don Richards had a place on the lake's north shore, the Nevada side, and Leland, running low on gas, was running on the assumption that he still did. He turned left.

Kings Beach, California, could be described as bustling. "This place is bustling," Leland said to the dog. The street was lined with restaurants, souvenir shops, boutique motels, and motor lodges, especially on the lake side, and the community was populated with locals and tourists seeking sun and fun. Leland also noticed a number of families coming in and out of establishments, heading to or coming from the beach that welcomed one and all. It became less and less crowded as he made his way toward the Nevada state line and the historic Cal Neva Resort and Spa. Leland saw the sign, and his mind immediately went soaring back to trips he and either Mom, Dad, or all three had made to Tahoe. On family trips they seem to always stop at the Cal Neva because his father was amused by the fact that half the building was in California and the other half was in Nevada. A painted, black "state line" went right through the resort's outdoor swimming pool. Inside the California side was calm and sedate, while the Nevada side was always busy thanks to the slot machines and gaming tables.

Chester told Leland on more than one occasion that the place was once owned in the early 1960s by Frank Sinatra, who built a showroom *in* it and a helicopter landing pad *on* it. Old Blue Eyes performed and palled around with Dean Martin, Sammy Davis Jr., Marilyn Monroe, Joe DiMaggio, and other stars of that era before losing his gaming license after Chicago mobster Sam Giancanna was spotted wandering around the grounds. Leland was fascinated but never wondered why his dad was so interested and knowledgeable about the Cal Neva's certainly celebrity, somewhat shady past. His dad never bothered to tell him that the historic place employed both of Leland's paternal grandparents.

North Lake Boulevard became Lakeshore Drive when the road wound its way from one state to the next, and the name change was fitting. Leland could now see the brilliant blue waters of the world's largest alpine lake. Between the Jeep and the lake Leland knew were hidden driveways leading to million- and multimillion-dollar homes with lakefront addresses and views. Another, this time more personal, memory pushed its way to the front as he recalled a college girl whose parents owned one of the ritzy residences along the road. Leland smiled as he remembered being there twice, once with the girl's parents in attendance and once without. He also tried to remember the girl's name—it was Mariel or Margaret, something that starts with an *M*—but it wouldn't come. What did come flooding back was the memory of liking her a lot, a lot more as it turned out than either she or her parents liked him. "Madeline," he said out loud, and the pup popped her head up.

Out the driver's side window, he saw the mountainside littered with slightly less spectacular homes and cabins that, if built high enough, overlooked not only the roadway but also the lake. It was in this general area that Leland knew Snoshu's cabin once stood. He hoped it still did and that Don Richards was still the owner and occupant. But once again his memory was soft around the edges, and he couldn't place the exact location of the dwelling or the best route to its driveway. He turned off the main drag and onto Red Cedar Drive, hoping some landmark would bring the entire memory into clearer focus. The dog lay back down in the back of the Jeep when he slowed and turned. Turning off Red Cedar and trying Ponderosa Drive, then Silvertip Drive, took Leland past dozens of places—some impressive, some simple, but none he recognized as Snoshu's. He also remembered a two-tiered pier where he would sit in the sun watching friends, the girls clad in bikinis, jump off the top deck into the frigid, crystal-clear water. While pretending he liked sitting under the sun's blinding, blistering rays, he also pretended he wasn't afraid to join them in jumping, but in reality he was scared shitless. Every once in a while he mustered up the courage to jump anyway, hating every falling, floating, stomach-in-his-throat second. He could see the pier clearly in his mind but couldn't locate it out the window. He sensed it was down there, along the water's edge, somewhere close by.

THOSE DAYS

"You have got to stop doing that," Chester heard his mother tell his father. "Sooner or later they're going to catch you, and I don't want to think about what happens then."

"I'm very careful," said his dad. "I only take one or two at a time and only when the tables are really busy."

"You'll stop when they install the cameras in the ceiling—that I heard Sarah and some of the other girls talking about."

"That's a fact!" he heard his dad answer. He also heard what sounded like a light slap, hand to someplace soft. "But until that day comes, I'll keep being careful."

Chester loved listening in on his parents. It was one of the few times he actually felt close to the two of them. From his secret perch near the stairs, he could hear every word they said when both were in the kitchen. He felt like a spy, a little. He knew they were talking about his dad's dangerous habit of stealing chips from the casino. He had seen some of the stash when he "cracked" his dad's safe. He nodded his head, agreeing silently with his mother. He wanted his dad to stop stealing from his workplace too. It wasn't because of some moral high ground or because he knew stealing was bad. He wanted him to stop because he feared if his dad got caught with his hand in the till, other people who worked for the bosses would do very bad, very mean things to him. On several occasions he had counted the chips in the safe and knew for a fact that it wouldn't be enough money to pay for either the hospital or the funeral. While he contemplated that not-so-sanguine future, his father spoke again.

"Big Man says the boss signed some songbird and her sisters to perform in the showroom. He heard talk about a special show for employees only, and I think we should go." Chester knew Big Man was his "uncle" Jeff, his dad's coworker and best friend. When he was just a kid, he thought Jeff was his real uncle. As he got older, he learned his dad was an only child, but he still kept calling Jeff "Uncle Jeff" anyway. He did have a real uncle and an aunt, Matt and Matilda, "Tilly," on his mom's side of the family, but they lived in Florida, so he never saw them. He did get a one-dollar bill inside a funny card from each on his birthday, so he liked them for that.

"Who's the singer?" his mother asked his father, interrupting Chester's family-tree train of thought.

"Some eleven-year-old kid named Frances Gumm, or so says the Big Man. Claims the big bosses called her a helluva talent. Goes on stage with a couple of sisters." For the next several seconds, Chester heard nothing, and then his dad spoke again, in a stern voice, this time from right behind him.

"How long you been sitting there?"

Chester spun around on his rear end, scared to death. *So much for being a spy,* he thought.

"Just a couple of minutes," he lied. "Long enough to hear you talking about Uncle Jeff and some girl singer named Gunn."

"Gumm," his father said as stern turned to something close but not quite a smile, "Frances Gumm. Maybe, if you're lucky, you can come hear her sing too." Chester nodded his head slowly, in approval of the idea, but he knew deep down he was rarely lucky. "Now get on up to bed or the deal's off." Chester obeyed, but on its surface, his dad knew it was an order without a real consequence.

The boy was on his back, in bed, thinking about Frances Gumm. The room was bathed in blue-black nonlight. In his right hand, he rubbed the smooth piece of white bone his dad's friend "Big Man" had given to him. He had called it scrimshaw. Chester had a bad habit of biting his fingernails, and his mother wanted him to stop. He wanted that too. Maddeningly everything she tried to help him was unsuccessful, including putting Tabasco sauce on his nails. Turned out he actually liked the spicy, red liquid. Then his "uncle" came up with the scrimshaw idea. He gave it to Chester after he had heard about the nail-biting dilemma, claimed it came from the inside of a whale. The boy laughed out loud at that one but kept the talisman, and then he looked it up and found out his dad's friend was telling the truth.

"Just rub it," the adult had instructed, "you know, every time you feel like putting your grubby little fingers in your mouth." Chester laughed again, but he did it and it worked. As his thumb worked one side and his forefinger the other, his thoughts returned to the young singer. He vowed to find out more about this—what had his dad called her? Oh yeah, "songbird"—who was close to his age. He put down the scrimshaw, clicked on his bedside lamp, and then reached for the book by its side. He picked it up and looked at the spine despite knowing exactly what it was, Honore de Balzac. He couldn't explain it, but he liked the seventeenth-century French guy, even though Chester struggled to understand a lot of what he wrote. He flipped the pages until he found the dog-eared one that contained the words the boy liked best: "The secret of great fortunes without apparent cause is a crime forgotten, for it was properly done." He repeated the words over and over to himself as he drifted off to sleep.

THESE DAYS

All the reminiscing had taken his mind off the fact that neither he nor Potter had anything to eat or drink since early that morning. His stomach suddenly took control and reminded him of that with a rumble. So before resuming his search for old friends, older dwellings, and new answers, he decided to grab a bite and get settled in his temporary accommodations. Leland had a ton of acquaintances but few true friends. The ones that were, were good ones. Jeremy Porter was among them. The two had met in college and found common ground around baseball after separately joining an intramural slow pitch softball league on the same day. Leland was a pitcher and a San Francisco Giants fan, while Porter played shortstop and loved the New York Yankees. Each respected the other and found the competition invigorating, the conversation interesting, and the friendship enduring.

It was months before either knew the other had more money than most, and neither much cared after making the discovery. Leland's money had trickled down from father to son, while his friend Jeremy made his millions all by himself. Porter had grown up a skier on the slopes of the Sierra Nevada Mountain Range and, in his "spare" time as a teenager, invented a contraption that could play his favorite music while he mastered the moguls. He figured out a way to take a simple car stereo cassette tape player, power it with a battery, attach headphones and tuck it in a padded case that he strapped to his chest. Sanyo, SONY, Motorola, and others loved the idea and approached the young entrepreneur with offers. He accepted one and then took some of that money and invested it in a company called Hayes Communication that was developing something called a modem.

Around the same time, Leland David was dreaming of drool thimbles and investing some of his not-so-hard-earned money in briefcase alarm technology. The concept behind the case was simple. When a businessperson's briefcase was swiped, a remote-control trip switch would trigger an alarm and send off a signal to release billows of red smoke from the pilfered piece of property. All well and good—until during testing, it was revealed that while the owner of the briefcase would most likely get his or her property back, everything inside said case would be covered in and ruined by the chemicals. As Leland would say to Jeremy about a number of things over a cold beverage on countless occasions, "It seemed like a good idea at the time."

With his well-earned wealth, Porter had purchased a second—or was it a third or a fourth?—home in the Lake Tahoe North Shore community of Incline Village. Some locals called it Income Village, and as Leland closed in on the left turn that would lead him to Porter's driveway, it was easy to see why. Parts of wooden decks, sections of huge windows, and glimpses of giant spider-web-shaped satellite dishes could be seen through the trees. As in most affluent communities, the people on the inside wanted to be able to observe the ones on the outside but not vice versa. It bothered Leland less here because somebody he cared about was one of the insiders. That and the fact that it was so damn beautiful. Two left turns later, Leland pulled into the driveway, popped the glove box, and pulled out the garage door opener Jeremy had given him years before.

The pup had set paws in the lake house on just one prior occasion, but she had no trouble finding a sun-splashed spot on the hardwood floor smack in the middle of a massive picture window—one of many that allowed a magnificent view of pine trees, mountains, and the icy-blue waters of the lake below. Leland tossed his canine companion her latest favorite chew toy and set out to making himself equally comfortable.

THOSE DAYS

hester sat in the dimly lit alley, eyes on the mom-and-pop store he had just robbed. He smiled and stared at the light and rubbed the piece of scrimshaw with the fingers of his right hand, white sugar dust from the stick of pink baseball-card bubble gum between the fingers of his left. He was dressed head to toe in black, including his brand-new Chuck Taylor Converse All-Star shoes, which he had transformed from white to black with a Marks-A-Lot. His mom would be mad, but his dad wouldn't care.

"Leave the kid alone," he knew his pop would say because he had said it a hundred times before. He would probably even add, "You baby him too much. Let him be a kid." He had said that before too. Both his parents were casino workers, leaving Chester alone with plenty of time to study, watch TV, and learn things beyond regular schoolwork that he figured he needed to know. One of the things he taught himself was how to crack a safe.

His dad had a small one, safe that is, and thought he had it hidden, but Chester found it one day after school behind a row of black slacks and white shirts in the bedroom closet. It intrigued him, left him wondering about its contents. It was made by the Mosler Safe Company of Hamilton, Ohio. Said so right on its black door. The letters were just above a numbered dial and a handle, set side by side. The dial said Mosler too and looked a little like the Master padlock he used to secure his locker at school, only bigger. He supposed it worked the same way, as well. He tried several combinations, including his and his parent's birthdays, with no success, and then he got creative.

One day he feigned an illness in class, earning a trip to the school nurse. Once inside the room, he pilfered a stethoscope and brought it home. As usual both his parents had already left for work by the time he made it home from school, so he made a beeline for the bedroom closet. Chester David was, by modern terminology, a latchkey kid—a label that, if he had known it growing up, would have made him laugh out loud. He used the medical instrument exactly the way the books he read described and the actors he watched in the gangster movies he loved had. He meticulously turned the dial, and when he heard the tumbler click into place for the very first time, Chester almost peed his pants. He had cracked his first safe and was both a little amused and slightly upset by its contents. His father had hidden away, among other things, several *Playboy* magazines, his and his wife's last will and testaments, a baseball autographed by Mel Ott, and what looked to be about a thousand dollars' worth of casino chips. The colorful cache of discs was of assorted denominations, but all bore the logo of the casino at which his father was employed.

Chester also taught himself how to pick a lock. He used both skills at least a couple of times a month to get into and out of Lander's Market after the mom-and-pop had closed up shop and retired for the evening. Most nights he took just one pack of baseball cards, never from the top of the box, and occasionally he grabbed two. He also took all the cash inside the store's safe. He would then take his ill-gotten gains back into the alley where he would sit, open the pack, pop the gum into his mouth, and see which, if any, players he would be able to add to his bourgeoning collection. After spending some time with each player, examining the photo and reading the stats, he would put the keepers in his back pocket.

THESE DAYS

Leland was famished and had stopped at Ahhh Capicola, a sandwich shop that caught his attention. The inside of the tiny delicatessen was as interesting as he had hoped. A slight smile crossed his lips upon entering and hearing music, sans instrumental accompaniment, softly exiting the speaker system. As pleasing as that was to his sense of hearing, his sense of smell was even more tantalized. His nose was filled with the scents of oregano, oil, vinegar, and freshly baked bread. His stomach grumbled, his mouth watered, and his eyes went straight to the "Barbershop Quartet" sub, listed first on the giant menu board plastered on the wall above the cash register. The "quartet" in the sandwich was capicola, Genoa salami, prosciutto, and provolone cheese. Red leaf lettuce, sliced fresh tomatoes, olive oil, white-wine vinegar, and flakes of oregano, dried basil, and crushed red pepper were added at his request. It was all stuffed inside a sliced, fresh-from-the-oven Italian roll, cut in half and then wrapped in white butcher paper. He would have devoured it on the spot, but he hated to leave the dog waiting in the car, and Jeremy's house was mere moments away, so he accepted a pickle on the side, told the girl behind the counter he'd grab a Dr. Pepper on the way out, and paid for his lunch.

Back at the "cabin," Leland laid out the contents of his lunch bag on the granite counter atop a massive island in the gourmet kitchen.

After taking a sip from the still-quite-cold soda pop, he tore into the sandwich, and the first bite was as delicious as he had hoped it would be. For the next few minutes, his attention was focused solely on satisfying his hunger and thirst. That done, he decided to put his belongings in one of the upstairs bedrooms and refamiliarize himself with the house. The dog didn't care in which room her master dropped his suitcase but was more than willing to join him as he started to look around. He scratched the pup behind her right ear and walked into the great room. Impeccably decorated, the space included a big-screen TV, chairs, couches, a thirty-two-inch hand-papered, illuminated, standing globe, a jukebox, a Space Invaders video game, and posters, paintings, and pictures on the wall. Potter plopped down and gave her right front paw a lick, while Leland moved in to get a closer look at some of the framed pictures on display. One that caught his eye showed a smiling Jeremy with his right arm around an equally happy looking, athletic, and stunningly beautiful woman. Kelli Meachem was Jeremy's girlfriend at the time—now she was his wife and, thanks to that happenstance, Leland David's friend.

He had been around Kelli on a few random occasions before the Porter/Meachem nuptials, and each had found the other not only acceptable but also pleasant company. All three shared common ground on several subjects including sports (they all played golf and loved football and baseball), red wine, and political philosophy. But Leland and Kelli agreed on things that Jeremy either didn't care about or didn't care enough about to offer up an opinion. So two-thirds of the group thought *Monty Python and the Holy Grail* was at or near the top of the funniest movies ever made and The Beatles were far superior to The Rolling Stones. Kelli and Leland also saw eye to eye on the belief that lyrics were more important than melody in determining a great song, and she impressed the socks off Leland one night when she proved she knew all the words to both Barry Manilow's "Looks Like We Made It" and Rob Base's "It Takes Two." Jeremy made it all three when it came to liking country music but again had a difference of opinion when it came to naming the most optimistic song ever written. Leland cast his vote for George Harrison's "Here Comes the Sun," while Jeremy, whether sober or drunk, always argued for Harold Melvyn and the Blue Notes's "Wake Up Everybody." Much to the embarrassment of both boys, Kelli held tightly to her belief that "Tomorrow" from the Broadway musical *Annie* trumped them all.

"We've had some good times, girl," Leland said aloud to the puppy and the framed photo as he petted the top of the Berner's head.

He continued to move through the house reminiscing and reconstructing some of the best days of his life, but he never forgot the reason for the Tahoe trip in the first place, to get answers about exactly who and what his father was. He made sure Potter had food and water.

"Be a good girl," he said to the dog, and he headed out the door.

THOSE DAYS

It was getting late, and Chester knew, even though no one was there waiting, he should be getting home. He had been in the corner of the library, studying, so quiet and still that the librarian hadn't even seen him when she got up from her desk, picked up her purse, and walked out the door. With the flick of a switch and the click of a lock, she left Chester alone in the dark. Holding his breath, he watched her go, delighted in the thought of being invisible. He turned back to the book in his hands. He was still there, reading in the same position, when the door opened sometime later and the janitor walked in, pulling a cart filled with cleaning supplies behind him. He flipped on the lights and immediately noticed the young man sitting in the corner.

"Chester?"

The no-longer-invisible Chester David looked up from the pages, smiled, and answered back, "Hello, Mr. Lewis."

"What are you still doing here? Everybody else is long gone, and you should be too."

"I know," the young man answered. "I just wanted to finish this book so I could get started on my book report. I was sitting here quietly, and Mrs. Green must have forgot about me," he said proudly. "She just left!"

"*Forgotten*," the janitor corrected.

"What?"

"*Forgotten,*" Mr. Lewis repeated. "She must have *forgotten* about you, not forgot about you."

"Oh, right, forgotten," Chester repeated, and made the mental note.

This wasn't the first time the custodian and the child had crossed paths after the final school bell had rung. Chester hung around school quite often, and Mr. Lewis had come across him in the library as well as a random hallway or classroom before. The boy was always reading a book or writing or drawing on a piece of paper. The janitor knew from the moment he laid eyes on him that he wasn't a vandal or a troublemaker, but there was something slightly unsettling about the kid. Despite that, he liked the boy and was never upset when he turned a corner or flipped on a light and discovered Chester and his bag of supplies.

"What are you reading?" He grabbed the broom and starting to sweep the library floor.

"*The Return of Sherlock Holmes,*" Chester answered, without looking down at the book, "*The Adventure of the Empty House.*"

"I love Sherlock Holmes." Mr. Lewis was sweeping and smiling.

"I like Moriarty." The boy also smiled.

The janitor shook his head and spoke again. "You ought to get on home, Chester."

"I know, sir." He closed the book and rose to his feet. He put it on top of a small stack of schoolbooks and picked them all up. "I'm going." And he did.

On his way out of the school building, he heard a noise coming from the gymnasium. It was a rhythmic thumping, like someone hitting or kicking a heavy bag. Curious, Chester broke his recent promise and followed the noise. After several more steps, he stopped at the gym and continued to hear the noise. He opened one of the double doors a crack and, with his right eye, peered in. He could see most of Coach Carmichael, the PE teacher, dressed in what looked to Chester like a white bathrobe, alternately hitting and kicking a large black leather bag hanging on a hook. The coach leaned back and kicked the bag with his bare right foot and then stood straight up, spun around, and began attacking the bag with his hands. A right jab was followed by another right and then a left—all to the same spot on the dark leather. Chester was fascinated and wanted a better look, so he tried quietly to open the gym door a little wider. The door opened slightly but not silently. An old hinge squealed as Chester attempted to open the wooden door another inch or two.

"Gotta tell Mr. Lewis to oil that," Chester said under his breath.

"Who's there?" Coach Carmichael said out loud.

Chester opened the door all the way, accompanied by another squeal, and stepped inside the gym.

"It's me, Chester, Coach. Chester David."

"David?" What on earth are you still doing here? And why are you sneaking around like a delinquent?"

"I'm not. I didn't mean to." He was a little afraid of Coach Carmichael. "I was in the library reading, and Mr. Lewis kicked me out." Chester started babbling. "I was heading out and heard a noise coming from the gym, so I decided to take a look. What are you doing?"

"Slow down, son." The coach smiled and took a couple of big steps toward the boy. Chester froze, wanting to turn and run but unable to get his legs to move. Coach Carmichael was now a few feet in front of him.

"It's called Bartitsu." He assumed a martial-arts stance, assuming Chester would have no idea what he was talking about. He was wrong. Chester's eyes widened.

"Like in the Sherlock Holmes book!" he said excitedly. "Bartitsu! It's what Holmes says he used to kill Moriarty at Reichenbach Falls."

"What?" The stunned coach stared at the kid.

"Never mind." A smile formed on Chester's face. "Can you teach me? I mean, could you please teach me, sir?"

Even more curious about the young man than before, the coach paused and then said, "Sure, I guess. Why not?" He turned and walked back to the bag with Chester hot on his heels.

THESE DAYS

Four establishments and two very cold, very dry Hendricks Gin martinis later, Leland had a nice little buzz going but very little in the way of new information. What he did know was that he was on a wild-goose chase, stopping at random watering holes, looking for any information about a character named Don "Snoshu" Richards. He felt like a creep or a bad private eye or both and had received nothing more than a few strange glances and a couple of overpriced drinks. As he got off his stool to leave, he checked his phone and found he had neither a voice nor text message. He didn't know why he even bothered to check since an earlier conversation with Jeremy had informed him that both his friend and his friend's wife, Kelli, were exploring other parts of the globe and wouldn't be returning to Tahoe for weeks, at least. But even though he knew there was no urgency in his search, he couldn't get over the unsettling feeling that urgency did, in fact, exist.

Leland walked out of the bar into the dimming light of another day gone. To his left was his car and the three bars he had already visited. To his right was one more watering hole. He went right. The sign next to the door was rather small but new and, upon further inspection, relatively nuanced. It depicted a baseball catcher, in full gear, squatting as if to receive a fastball. Instead of a batter's box, the player was positioned inside a glass of golden brown liquid. Intrigued, and up for one more martini, Leland opened and walked through the door.

THOSE DAYS

ometimes Chester walked to school, but mostly he rode his bike. He had gotten a used Murray bike for Christmas. He thought it was really cool at first, but soon found out it wasn't "up to snuff" when compared to the Schwinn and AMF bikes parked next to his at school. He was informed of his bike's shortcomings every now and then by some of the less sensitive kids at school, and almost every day by the mean ones, like Marty Moran. Chester was home from school, in the driveway one day, when his dad pulled up in the car just after getting off a casino shift. Dressed in his customary black slacks and white shirt, he carried his tie in his right hand and stopped and put his left hand on Chester's shoulder. The child knew what would happen next. His father would ask him a couple of questions, pretending to be interested but not really caring. It used to bother the boy but not anymore.

"Hi, pal." His voice and smile were tired. "Whatcha doin'?"

"Hi, Dad." Chester didn't look up from his task. "Just putting some new cards in the spokes."

His dad stood and watched as Chester, with a wooden clothespin, attached an ace of spades to the spokes of the bike's front wheel. Cards between the spokes made a clacking noise when the wheels turned, and the faster you rode the louder the noise became. Kids had done it in Chester's dad's youth, and they were still doing it in

Chester's. He hadn't taught his son that; in fact in that very moment, he wondered if he had taught his son anything.

"Want to play catch later?" he asked, both of them knowing it would never happen. Chester wasn't a big kid, but his father had noticed early on that he had great hand-eye coordination and some days he would observe, from the comfort of his favorite chair, his son spending hours practicing his technique, throwing a tennis ball against the garage door. Other days his dad would find him pouring through an Encyclopedia Britannica or a random *LIFE* magazine, studying the perfect way to throw a curveball or a fastball. To his amazement the kid could translate what he gleaned on paper to an actual grip or throwing motion that resulted in what appeared, from that same comfortable chair and distance, to be perfect strikes. The kid was a quick study, thought the father. He also thought the boy, his boy, was a little odd.

"Sure," Chester was resigned to the fact that it would probably be the last time he saw his dad until dinner and attached a king of hearts. His dad, knowing it too, headed for the house, not looking back and without another word.

Next Chester clipped the queen of clubs to a spoke and smiled. He liked being able to amuse, entertain, and take care of himself. He guessed he loved his mom and dad, even though he was pretty darn sure other kids had better ones. He really liked his bike, even though he was positive there were prettier, more expensive ones. Kids at school, like that jerk, Moran, made sure to let him know it, but he didn't care. This one was perfect for him. But he told himself, flat-out promised, if and when he had a kid of his own, he would give him the best of everything.

THESE DAYS

Inside, the establishment was reasonably well lit and relatively empty. Leland's arrival upped the occupancy level by 25 percent, and that included the bartender. She was positioned behind what looked to be a clean, instantly inviting bar with an assortment of bottles and glasses on her side. Wooden stools with backs were on his. She stood next to the cash register. He stood, taking in the scene, liking how it all felt, what he saw around the room, and behind the bar. Then he, as they used to say someplace, sometime, bellied up. The girl behind the bar had yet to look up, like she was used to people walking through the door, even though the number of people inside on a Friday night suggested otherwise. Leland noticed she wore a plain white T-shirt (no logos, no stains) and extremely well-fitting blue jeans. He guessed her light brown hair was slightly longer than shoulder length. He had to guess because it was pulled back in a very tight ponytail. Leland tried not to stare as he wondered who first called that particular style a "ponytail." The look made the why obvious, but he still thought about whether or not it was initially used as a complimentary description.

"Can I get you something, or did you just wander into my bar to stare?" She was no longer not paying attention to him. Her voice sounded as good as she looked, and it brought Leland out of his reverie, gently. "Sorry. I wasn't aware I was staring," he answered truthfully. "I was just wondering about the origin of the term *pony-tail*." He stopped for a second and then added, "Not yours specifically, just in general." Then he smiled.

"That's a new one," she said under her breath but still just loud enough for Leland to hear. Then she smiled back and asked, "What can I get you?"

"A really cold, really dry Hendricks martini, up with one olive." He watched as she turned to grab the distinctive bottle off the shelf and started to prepare the cocktail.

THOSE DAYS

Chester actually liked and respected Mr. and Mrs. Lander. They had always been kind to him, and he had watched them be kind to dozens of other kids too. But there were plenty of preteens and teenagers who didn't deserve the Landers' kindness. The couple had owned the store for decades, and Chester guessed kids underestimated them because they were old, "maybe even pushing sixty" he'd overheard classmates say. Those same classmates felt that old age made the Landers an easy target for shoplifting, and occasionally they tried to do just that. Some got away with it, but most weren't so fortunate. When Mom or Pop Lander pounced on one of them trying to pick their pocket by stuffing a candy bar, handful of bubble gum, or pack of baseball cards into a purse, coat, or pair of jeans, the punishment was swift and severe. One of the proprietors would seemingly appear out of nowhere and strike, grabbing the ear of the thief with one hand and retrieving the merchandise with the other. Next, earlobe in hand, they would lead the blubbering bandit out the front door. They would never call the parents if it was a first-time offense. That fate was saved for a second attempt. If you were brazen or brainless enough to try a third time, then local law enforcement entered the picture. First-time offenders didn't get off scot-free; in fact, the punishment for them was cruel indeed: banishment from the establishment for two weeks, and for some that was worse than having their parents informed.

Each time he watched some howling hoodlum beg Mr. or Mrs. Lander not to call their parents, Chester thought two things. First, that one of his own folks would be mortified but the other wouldn't care, and second, that he would always be smart enough not to get grabbed by the ear. Sitting in the alley across from the establishment, he glanced at the Timex on his wrist and waited. Seconds later a local PD car cruised past on the way to the neighborhood diner. Chester knew that's where it was headed because he had followed the cop car on his bike every night for a week, and that's where it always ended up. He waited another forty-five seconds exactly and then rose to his feet, walked over to the front of the store, and picked the lock for the second time that night. Then he did what he did every single time. He put back every single penny he had taken from the Lander's safe.

THESE DAYS

"How's the martini?" She surprised him because he had just been thinking how delicious it was compared to the others he had drunk in the bars down the street.

How is that possible? he thought to himself as he said out loud, "It's pretty good."

"It's *pretty* good?"

Oh my God, he thought again as he raised the martini glass to his lips in hopes of hiding whatever he was certain his face was betraying at that moment.

"Yup. Pretty darn good," he managed between sips and discreetly tried to look for a wedding ring on her left hand. He found no jewelry in sight, save for a small diamond *D* on a thin chain around her neck. Of course, no ring meant absolutely nothing these days, Leland thought.

"You're staring again," she said, touching the D and then grabbing the towel on her shoulder and walking away to wipe down the other end of the bar.

"Geez," Leland said, loudly enough for her to hear, "just thinking again." The unnecessary clean up started to bring her closer to his spot at the bar.

THOSE DAYS

Chester had been arriving early or staying after school for weeks, but instead of heading for the library or some other quiet place to read or do homework, he'd make a beeline for the gym. Coach Carmichael was tutoring the young man on Bartitsu, and Chester turned out to be a quick study. The coach found the boy to be fast, nimble, and smart. The student was picking up the moves almost faster than the teacher could introduce them.

"You're good at this," Coach Carmichael would say as Chester threw another right fist at the black bag. "Much stronger and more athletic than I imagined you would be."

"Thanks. I think." They both would chuckle.

Chester walked through the halls of the school, thinking about the martial art and looked forward to another session later that day. He assumed his usual hallway posture, head down, backpack bouncing, and avoiding eye contact with the other kids. Suddenly something slammed into his left shoulder, spinning Chester around and knocking him to the ground. A couple books tumbled out of his pack. Shoulder throbbing, he reached out in an attempt to gather them. A big, sneakered foot stepped on his outstretched fingers.

"Hey, dipstick! Watch where you're going!"

Chester looked up to see a shit-eating grin on the pudgy face of Marty Moran. From the ground he also saw Moran was surrounded by a few of his faithful followers—toadies who had no idea how embarrassing they looked, looking up to the school bully.

"Sorry," Chester said insincerely. "Could you please get off my hand?" he added sincerely.

"Is that your *hand*?" the bully spat. "I thought it was a bug." He cackled at what he perceived was a joke. His minions tried to parrot the awful sound but failed miserably. Moran stepped off. Then, with his left hand, he reached down and grabbed Chester by the shirt collar, while one of his stooges scooped up the books that had spilled out of Chester's bag. He put them in the bully's right hand. At one time, not all that long ago, Chester would have been truly afraid but not anymore. He was rattled, for sure, but determined not to show it. Moran lifted both the boy and the books, dangling Chester a few inches off the ground and eyeing one of the volumes.

"Ball Sack?" screamed the bully in Chester's face. His breath smelled like sour milk, cigarettes, and stupidity. "What the heck? Who the hell is Ball Sack?"

"It's Balzac." Chester emphasized the z.

"Did I tell you to talk?" Moran snarled and pulled the smaller boy closer. "Did I tell him to talk?" He turned and asked his flunky friends. While they shook their heads, Chester quickly and silently lifted both hands then brought them back to his sides, the movement unseen by Moran, his gang, or any of the other students who had started to gather.

"What's going on here?" a voice boomed. "Don't all of you have someplace you're supposed to be?" The crowd dispersed, revealing Coach Carmichael with his arms crossed. He eyed Moran, who still had a hold of both the boy and his books, and shook his head. Then he turned his gaze to Chester, who gave him a slight, almost imperceptible smile.

"Put the kid down, Mr. Moran," the adult said slowly, making sure the big dope understood every word, "and give him back his books."

Moran looked at the coach for a second or two longer than he should have, finally looking back at what he still thought of as his prey, still dangling a few inches off the ground.

"Next time watch where you're going, wimp!" He released Chester and dropped the books back down to the linoleum floor. "Let's go, guys." Moran waved for his crew to step in line behind him. "I need a smoke." On the way out, one of the bully's boys gave Chester's book a little kick. It was Coach Carmichael who picked it up.

"Balzac, huh?" He handed the book back to his martial-arts pupil. "You OK?"

"Yes, sir, thank you, sir."

"You are quite an interesting cat, David." The coach said it in a complimentary way, then added, "Something tells me you would have been just fine even if I had never happened by."

"Maybe, sir." Chester looked the coach in the eye. "But thanks just the same."

"See you later, Chester." The coach walked away, waving.

Chester seethed as he put his books back in his backpack and looked up and down the hallway. Life had returned to normal, with students going both ways heading to their lockers or classrooms. Chester seethed as he walked to his own locker, stopped, spun the dial to his Master padlock, and opened the door. He set the backpack inside and reached into his pants pockets, pulling out the wallet he had snatched from the bully while he was otherwise occupied impressing his easily impressible buddies. Chester found he had mixed emotions about stealing the stuff, but he was quite proud of himself for being able to pull it off without being noticed. He grabbed the books he needed for class, shut the locker door, clicked, and then spun the lock. On the way to English class, he used his forefinger and thumb to pluck all eleven dollars from the bully's billfold then dropped the wallet in a hallway trash can, wondering if Mr. Lewis would discover it later on.

He had taken something from the bully—eleven dollars in wrinkled, dirty bills—but that in no way compensated for everything Chester perceived Marty Moran had taken from him. His pride. His dignity. Chester thought about the manhandling he had received at the hands of the bigger, dumber boy—couldn't stop thinking about it the rest of the day. It made him sad; it made him angry. It hurt him from the inside out. He *hated* Marty Moran, and he wanted him to hurt too.

Coach Carmichael had set up a special room so that he, Chester, or both, could practice and train in relative peace. It was once a large equipment closet filled with various balls from basket to dodge to foot, as well as jump ropes, wrestling mats, and track hurdles. The coach had gotten permission to relocate all of it and create this private space. At the moment Chester was in it.

There was a heavy bag hanging in the center, a much smaller speed bag off to one side, and various bricks, boards, and books on shelves. When a still stinging Chester entered on this day, he noticed several new additions on the far wall. Framed pictures of what looked to him like Chinamen—some bald, some bearded. Enveloped in a heavy cloak of anger, he thought no more about them and began attacking the heavy bag. He was there about twenty minutes when Coach Carmichael opened the door and joined him.

"Mr. David," the coach always addressed his pupil calmly and formally when they worked together in this space. Chester either ignored him or didn't hear him and pounded the bag again.

"Mr. David," he said again. The only response was the solid slap of a schoolboy's right foot on the bag.

"*Chester!*"

Chester stopped. The student hadn't been ignoring the teacher; he'd had no idea he wasn't still alone. Realizing he had company, he bowed deeply. The coach noticed the child's hair was damp with sweat and his cheeks were wet with tears. He returned the bow, and then they stood facing each other.

"Why are you training in your street clothes?" Chester looked down at himself and became suddenly aware that he hadn't changed into his Bartitsu gi. His face reddened, but he didn't offer an explanation or ask for forgiveness.

"Stevie Jameson told me a person could kill somebody by punching them in the nose with the palm of their hand. He wiped a wayward dribble of snot from his upper lip with the back of his left hand. "Said the bone would go right into the brain. Is *that* true?"

The coach stood stunned. "It's actually cartilage." He couldn't help correcting. "And *why* on earth would anyone want to do that?"

"Is it *true?*" Chester asked again as an answer. The coach inhaled and expelled a deep breath.

"What exactly is troubling you, son?" He attempted to change the subject. "Let's sit down and talk about *that* instead."

"No, thanks." Chester dismissed the notion and turned to deliver another blow to the bag. "Who are the Chinamen on the wall?" He was the one changing the subject after the perfectly executed thump. The coach marveled at how proficient the boy had become in such a short time. He was precise, purposeful, and, up until this latest exhibition, placid. For the first time, Carmichael saw a darkness he hadn't noticed before. An aura of anger that he felt had potential to consume the boy. That concerned him.

"Confucius, the Dalai Lama, and Sun Tzu." He pointed left to right. "And they aren't all Chinese."

"Huh." Chester didn't really care. "Can any of them kill a guy with one punch?"

"Probably." The coach did care. "But they never, *ever* would."

Chester tilted his head ever so slightly and regarded the coach. He grabbed his shoes in one hand then wiped away what was left of the sweat and tears. He took one last look at the men on the wall as he strode past the coach and out the door.

"Look them up!" the teacher called after his student.

THESE DAYS

"**A**bout what this time? Bangs? Perms?" the bartender chided.

Now it was his turn to smile. "Actually I was wondering about the name on the sign next to the door." He set the glass on the napkin on the bar. "It's cool, but what in the world does it mean?"

She stopped wiping down the bar and continued walking his way until she stood right in front of him. He could smell her, see the soft blond fuzz of hair near her right ear, and started to fall further down the like-lust-love rabbit hole.

"It's the name of the bar," she said, somewhat conspiratorially, "Catcher in the Rye."

Leland pictured the ball player squatting inside the rocks glass and nodded slowly. "Nice."

He looked up, and his eyes found hers.

"My dad was a big fan of both baseball and J. D. Salinger's classic novel." She looked down at the bar and gave one spot another wipe.

"Your dad?" he asked.

"He bought this place a few years ago, made me his partner, then went and had a heart attack. I've been the owner, bartender, and chief bottle washer ever since."

"I'm sorry about your dad" was all he could think to say.

"Thanks" was all she could think to reply.

Leland polished off his martini, reached into his pocket for a twenty, pulled it out, and left it on the bar.

"So maybe I'll see you tomorrow," he sounded hopeful as he hopped off the chair and headed for the door.

"Maybe you will." She, equally hopeful, pocketed the twenty and watched the door close behind him.

THOSE DAYS

Chester was back at the Lander's, in the dark. He had already stopped at the row that was home to the baseball-card box, knelt down, and for the dozenth—or was it hundredth—time (he had stopped counting), he grabbed a pack from the middle of the box and stuffed it into the back pocket of his black jeans. Next he straightened up, and like a dancer who had practiced a move across a stage until she could do it with her eyes closed, he made his way silently, mindlessly, toward the safe.

Standing before it, he mentally congratulated himself on how good he was getting at opening the little box full of cash. He wondered how much more quickly he could do it or if the Landers, or someone else for the matter, had a bigger, different safe. How long it would take him to open that one. Maybe it was because he allowed himself this brief moment of contemplation, or maybe it was because he had traced and retraced these steps so many times before that the nerve endings had dulled and the heightened sense of awareness had dipped to an all-time low. Regardless of the reason, he never heard Emmett Lander approach, and thus figuratively jumped out of his skin when the thirty-three-inch, thirty-two-ounce Louisville Slugger baseball bat the old man was wielding came to rest on his right shoulder.

He wanted to scream or run or piss his pants, but he did none of that. Lander had done nothing more than silently and effectively announce his presence. *Why hasn't he hit me?* Chester wondered, and then the man who currently held Chester's life in his hands, along with a wooden baseball bat, spoke.

"Hey, kid."

He sounds almost friendly, Chester thought, trying like mad to read the situation.

"Watcha doin?" Lander spoke again, this time sounding more like the cat that caught the canary.

"Getting ready to open your safe," the canary replied. Chester figured, *Why lie?* He was caught red-handed, breaking and entering probably the least of his problems—a Louisville Slugger to the knee, ribs, or temple more than likely the worst. What good would adding some mealy-mouthed lie to the current predicament do? Seconds that seemed like ticks on a forever clock passed, but no part of Chester's body was forced to play the part of a Rawlings baseball. Finally, or at least it seemed like finally, Lander spoke again.

"Again?" was all he said.

"Sir?" was the question to the question Chester asked.

"You gonna pretend to rob me again?" Now Chester said nothing, but Lander was far from finished. "You are gonna open that safe in about ten seconds"—*Seven,* Chester thought, but didn't interrupt by saying—"pull out all the cash, take it across the street, and set a spell looking at the baseball cards you *also* swiped"—he tapped the barrel of the bat on Chester's right butt cheek—"and then you are gonna bring it all back, every dollar, and put it back in the safe just to do it all again in a couple of days or a week."

Chester felt the weight of the bat on his shoulder again and wondered if the time for his beating had finally come.

"Turn around." Chester noticed the order carried no anger. He turned and faced his captor.

"You're good," Lander said, looking squarely into Chester David's eyes.

"You knew?"

"I knew."

"All this time?"

"Not *all* this time, but for a long time."

Chester looked at his shoes, toes pointed toward each other, then let out a soft whistle, and shook his head. He looked up at Lander, who now rested the bat on his own shoulder.

"You think I'm good?" It came out childlike, hopeful.

"I think you're better than good." Lander smiled and added, "And I can make you great."

THESE DAYS

There were a lot of reasons why Leland liked living in the West—relatively no humidity, fewer people, and NFL football games started early and were over by 4:30 p.m. on Sunday. Life, for whatever reason, seemed simpler, at least that's how it felt sitting out on the deck of the Tahoe house, a steaming mug of coffee cradled in his hands. The sky was clear blue. The air was crisp, and the paper, which Jeremy had had delivered every morning, was waiting to be read.

The dog had had her breakfast and was ready for a morning walk, but that would have to wait. Leland was having a moment for himself. He took a whiff and then a sip of the coffee and set the mug on the deck. He couldn't decide if it tasted or smelled better. Then his thoughts turned back to his father. How could he have fooled so many people for so long? When Leland walked into his dad's dirty, not-so-little, secret attic stash, he found himself in a world of make believe, stories, and deception. He had stumbled upon the birthplace of a world of lies that pulled the wool over people's eyes for decades. But there was genius hidden there too. As far as Leland could tell, his father hadn't hurt anybody, and despite the fact that the gold mine was predicated on a lie, there were nuggets of truth to be found. His father had visited local restaurants, bed and breakfasts, and hotels and then, in his own words, written about and evaluated them with a very clever ranking system. The world beyond a two-or-three state radius also actually existed, but what was written in the pages of the *CDD Guides* was a yarn. An analysis begat from that sliver of truth and then expanded upon, magnified, and romanticized in Chester David's fertile mind. He was decidedly very good at the deception considering an editor, a publisher, and hundreds of thousands, if not millions, of people had believed him. He had the royalty checks in the bank and dozens of volumes of work sitting on bookshelves to prove it.

Leland took another sip of coffee. But why keep it from his only son? Who else knew? And was it all a sham to cover up something else, something far more nefarious? The last question was the one that dogged Leland most, and it hadn't even entered into his thought process until his mind started spinning through the mental images of the attic that he had committed to memory. It was like the old red View-Master handheld projector he had as a kid. It allowed him to work through the images, one by one, in his brain. Thousands of magazines, arranged chronologically, and crammed into box, after box, after box, after box. They were stored, spine showing, giving Chester, and ultimately Leland, the ability to read the name of the magazine, the volume number and the day, week, or month and year in which it was made available to the world. All of those magazines, filled with history and heartache, wonder and world news, having been read once, twice, or a dozen times, left lying there waiting to be read again. But as the mental images continued to scroll, Leland noticed that not all the magazines were side by side, not all of them were packed the same way. Several, instead, stood like sentinels, straight up, at attention, overlooking the box or boxes in which their numbered pages brethren rested.

Leland absentmindedly stroked the fur on the dog's back.

"Why were those magazines packed that way?" he asked the puppy, not expecting an answer. He didn't get one.

"Why were they standing up? What made them stand out?" The dog sat up, but upon realizing none of the words emanating from her master's mouth was *walk*, she plopped back down on the deck. Leland picked up the still-folded paper, slid off the rubber band, and perused the front page despite the fact that he knew it wouldn't reveal any of the answers to his questions. Before he discarded the first section and headed for the sports pages, something in black and white caught his eye and stopped him dead in his tracks. "Local Legend Hospitalized" was what the one-column-inch headline on the lower right corner of the first page read. The first paragraph of the story told Leland the "local legend" was Don "Snoshu" Richards, and the second paragraph said where Leland could find him.

"Uncle Don!" Leland practically shouted. The pup popped up again.

THOSE DAYS

"Do you want some more soup?" Mrs. Lander asked in a grandmotherly way. He did, real bad, but this was already bowl number two, and he didn't want to look like his mother never fed him or, worse, appear greedy.

"No thank you, ma'am." His mouth was mostly full of noodles.

"Don't speak with your mouth full of food, son." It was old man Lander, sounding much more serious than his wife. "You never want to do anything that might bring attention to yourself. Folks remember other folks who chew with their mouths open, smack their chewing gum…" He paused and looked at Chester for the first time since the boy had arrived earlier that evening. "Or speak with their mouths full of food." Chester just nodded and then waited for more food for thought.

"Invisible." The word floated out of Lander's mouth at no more than a whisper. "You want to be invisible," he added louder, but not much.

Chester closed his mouth, chewed silently, and started thinking. He started to feel like he went from not really having a father to having two. One, Coach Carmichael, was helping him learn how to fight, and the other, Mr. Lander, was preparing him to be a thief. Both were, in their own ways, teaching a teachable Chester David how to be the man that *the boy* hungrily wanted to be.

"Uh, Mrs. Lander?"

"Yes, dear?" The small, older woman turned with a smile and a twinkle in her eye that said she already knew what was about to come out of Chester's postswallow mouth. Mr. Lander looked at Chester as well, only hoping he also knew what the boy was about to say.

"Thank you for the soup, ma'am. It was delicious." Then he politely wiped his mouth with the paper napkin, slid his chair back noiselessly, got up, and placed his dishes in the sink. He lifted the bar on the faucet that turned on the tap and shifted it so the water turned more hot than cold.

Deep down Chester would have loved one more bowl of the tasty chicken noodle soup, but he thought better of it. He'd be a good boy, a polite boy. He'd even wash his dishes. Then a thought stopped him. *What kind of kid would do his own dishes? The kind who would stand out, be memorable.* And with that he hit the tap and shut the water off.

The old man had watched the entire episode in silence. *I'm going to enjoy teaching this one,* he thought, knowing the lessons had already started.

THESE DAYS

Leland knew a lot of people who hated hospitals. He knew why they felt that way but couldn't explain why he didn't feel the same. Sure, they smelled funny, like antiseptic mixed with misery, draped in a cloud of impending doom. But sprinkled in and around the medicinal odor, Leland sensed faith, hope, healing, and the constant presence of a lust and longing for life. It probably helped that he hadn't spent much time inside hospitals since neither parent needed one on their way from this life to whatever was next. Personally his visits were rare, never having broken a bone or needing surgery. He still had his tonsils and his appendix and was years away from a vasectomy or colonoscopy—he mentally knocked on wood as he approached the nurses' station. There were two behind the desk, both busy, so he waited.

He looked at his right hand and noticed, for the millionth time, the several-inches-long scar that ran down the bottom of his ring finger, through the joint, and into the top part of his palm. He absentmindedly rubbed the raised, rough skin with the top of his right thumb. He could still vividly remember how it got there, could almost feel the pain again as he relived the day. It was winter, snowing. He and some of his buddies were being assholes. School was done for the day, and they thought the best use of their poststudies time was to park themselves behind an embankment overlooking a busy street and hurl snowballs at passing cars.

It was a giggle fest, packing and pitching the clumps of snow, picking off a station wagon here or a Volkswagen there. Then the fun stopped when somebody, he never knew who, nailed the passenger side door of what looked like a brand-new BMW. Most of the drivers in the cars, once hit, just kept on going, but this one, this time, slammed on the brakes and opened the driver's side door. Leland was back there now—fully immersed in the memory, scared shitless and in full retreat. In this version of the recollection, he didn't see any of his friends running with him, only the chain link fence straight ahead and the freedom that waited on the other side. In full stride he approached the metal, left hand and right foot slamming into it simultaneously. He reached for the crisscrossed top with his right hand and used his left foot to help propel him over. Up and over he went, spinning with a half turn in midair, bracing for the landing. He had made it, at least most of him had. His right hand, more specifically the tender spot between his ring and middle finger stayed put, speared by the sharp metal points that marked the top of each X. In the split second that his feet hit the ground, the skin in, around, and between his two digits split wide open. Gravity brought the hand down while gushing blood and curiosity took it right back up to eye level. He couldn't see much beyond the deep-red, almost-purple liquid leaving his body, but what he could see, he swore was bone.

He felt a wave of nausea but didn't scream because he feared if he opened his mouth he would lose everything he had eaten that day. He started, instead, to run again, straight home. Once there he raced for the bathroom and tried his best to attach a handful of Band Aids, then wrapped his hand as tightly as he could in a small towel. He staggered to the bed and lay down. Eventually—Leland had no way of knowing how long he bled, dozing off and on while fighting the feeling of having to vomit—his mom came home from work. Dad was gone again, visiting some exotic place, doing research for his next restaurant or hotel review. When his mother found him lying in bed, she wondered aloud what was wrong. Then she saw the blood-soaked towel seeping onto the blood-soaked sheet, and she screamed. A trip to the hospital, a couple of hours, and dozens of stitches later, he was back home—this time on the couch, watching TV.

"Sir? Sir, can I help you?" It was one of the nurses behind the desk who shook Leland from his memories. "Are you OK? Is there something wrong with your hand?" *How long has she been trying to get my attention?* Leland thought.

"Not anymore." He looked up and into her eyes. "I'm looking for Don Richards. I was hoping to pay him a visit."

THOSE DAYS

The house—his house—seemed lighter, brighter, less suffocating lately. Even his parents gave off the unmistakable impression of being happier. Chester couldn't put his finger on exactly why but supposed the breathing room was directly correlated to the time he spent away from his two parents and with his two mentors. He was growing up, and whether or not they could reasonably lay claim to any responsibility for it, his parents were clearly less miserable around their son and each other. Chester didn't care. He also didn't tell them about anything that happened at the Lander's. His tightly kept secret ran the gamut from his burglary practice sessions to getting caught by the old man to the subsequent relationship that had blossomed. He kept it all to himself, not because he cared one bit about how his parents might react—that wasn't it at all. He harbored it like a criminal because, after all, he was becoming a criminal, and he wanted the relationship all to himself—well, to himself and Mrs. Lander, of course.

So it was in the couple's living room where he found himself on another evening. Another evening he had told his parents he would be at the gym with Coach Carmichael learning how to protect himself. He hadn't stopped the sessions with the coach; he just did that during the day—a study period here, an extra hour after school there. He had also long since stopped "learning" how to protect himself;

he had that part pretty well down. For quite some time, the work with Coach Eddie Carmichael had become all about learning how to control his breathing, his balance, and his mind. He was mastering the art of being "visible" at the right time and, in old man Lander's words, "invisible" when the time was right for that.

"Hey, kid." Lander addressed him in the now-familiar way. Chester looked up from his studies. The man was older than his dad, but Chester, for the life of him, had no idea by how much. He held a drink in one hand and his wife's tiny, incredibly strong hand in the other. Chester recognized both the color and the odor of scotch. The woman looked slightly younger than her husband, and Chester rambled through his mental dictionary for the right word before landing on *content*. The old man spoke.

"Can you tell me the perfect crime?"

Chester thought hard. *Was this a test?* Somewhere in the recesses of his still-developing brain he was sure he had an answer for this, but was it *the* answer? Had he read it in one of his Hardy Boys mysteries or a Sherlock Holmes story or did it come from another, disconnected place?

"I think I know the answer to this one!" he practically shouted when it came to him. For effect he took a sip of his hot chocolate— Mrs. Lander made delicious hot chocolate—and then offered his answer. "A lady offed her husband." The euphemism made both the husband and wife smile. "And then she cut him up, cooked him, fed the meat to her family, and gave the bones to the dog." He took a breath and another sip of the warm, chocolatey goodness. He was proud of himself and looked toward Mr. Lander for approval.

Mrs. Lander smiled warmly; Mr. Lander did not.

"It's the perfect crime." Chester was still sure of himself.

"What it is, is an entertaining tale." Mr. Lander sipped his scotch and regarded the boy, who regarded him back. "But wrong." Chester's shoulders slumped, and he opened his mouth to protest. Before any words could come out, Lander held up his hand, indicating the boy needn't bother.

"You're overthinking it, my young protégé." His smile was so kind it warmed the young boy's soul. He took another sip of the golden liquid that warmed his own. "The perfect crime is the one you get away with," he concluded, with a wink.

"A crime forgotten because it was properly done." Chester repeated the words from memory.

"Sounds like Balzac." Impressed, Lander lifted his glass.

THESE DAYS

Leland stood in the hospital room doorway. Visiting hours were almost over, but the nurse said he could stay for a few minutes to keep the patient company. Richards, she had said, mostly slept. That's what he was doing now as Leland watched. Machines glowed and beeped, sent readings, and dispensed medicine while Richards lay there, eyes closed, head slightly propped up by pillows.

"Uncle Don," Leland whispered. Richards wasn't blood, but he was the closest thing Leland had to it growing up. The prone patient was his dad's best friend, confidant, traveling companion, and major domo for as long as he could remember. His "uncle" was a large man who led a large life, and Leland had never heard one single person say a bad thing about him. Despite his popularity, Leland also recalled that Richards always treated his father with respect. In fact, it bordered on reverence. He took a step into the room, and, almost on cue, Don Richards opened his eyes. Unfocused at first, they found Leland, and a smile formed on his dry, chapped lips.

"Leebo," Richards rasped. He had called Leland by that nickname for as long as the young man could remember. It was the only name his "uncle" used to address him, and Don Richards was the only person on earth who called him that.

"Hello, Snoshu." Leland exchanged nicknames and took another step into the room. "It's good to see you."

"Before you get a closer look," Richards said, and slowly raised his right hand pointing a shaking finger at the bedside table, "could you pour me a cup of water?"

"No problem." Leland reached for the pink plastic pitcher and did as he was told.

After what felt like hours later, he was still there telling stories, catching up, asking a lot of questions, and getting a few answers. They were interrupted by an inconsistent parade of nurses and an occasional, impromptu "Snoshu Snooze." At some point in the conversation, Leland brought up discovering the magazines, comprehending his father's mendacity, and wondering what it all meant. Richards offered no answers or explanations, responding only occasionally with a slight nod, a head shake, and a wry smile. Finally, fully frustrated, Leland got out of his chair.

"I'm gonna go," he said, "but I'd like to come back. I'd really like to know what my dad was up to all those years. Maybe next time you'll be more forthcoming." It was statement, not a request.

"Son, wait." Richards touched his arm. The sincerity of his tone and the sensitivity of his touch made Leland wonder if the man was finally ready to give him some answers. "Before you go, could you hand me that pad and pencil on the table?" Disappointed, Leland again did as he was asked.

"Sit for one more minute," the older man implored, and then he began to write. After a few labored minutes, he signaled he had finished by dropping the pencil and tearing a sheet of paper from the pad. Appearing exhausted, he managed to fold the paper into a square and place it in the palm of Leland's hand. Then he closed his eyes and drifted off to sleep without saying good-bye.

For the second time in a few minutes, Leland lifted himself out of the hospital room chair, kissed Richards on the forehead, and walked out. Sitting in his car, in the parking deck, he finally opened his clenched left fist, plucked the note with his right, and unfolded the piece of now-crumpled paper. He took one deep breath and read what his uncle had written. Surprisingly the words appeared to be the product of a strong, steady hand. Not surprisingly they were cryptic.

>*don't be too hard on your old man. he was Doing the Best he Could. celebrate all the days of his life.*

And that was it. Leland shook his head. *Best he could?* He scoffed.

THOSE DAYS

"**D**o you have any friends, son?" Lander was reading the newspaper, spectacles perched at the very tip of his larger-than-normal nose. Chester was on the floor, in the prone position, as if he belonged there. He was doing his homework, his actual schoolwork—not the homework Lander continually gave him dealing with lock picking and safe cracking.

"What?"

Lander wondered if the boy really hadn't heard the question or if he was too embarrassed to answer it, so he asked again, "Do you have any friends?"

Mrs. Lander was suddenly in the room, taking the young man, but not the older one, by surprise.

"How do you do that?" Chester wondered, looking up at the little old lady.

"How do I do what, dear?" She answered with a question.

"Materialize, out of nowhere, just like that." Chester snapped his fingers. "One second you're not here, and the next second you are!" Chester snapped again. "And you never make a sound."

"Practice."

"Do you have any friends?" Mr. Lander asked for a third time, paying no attention to the comings and goings of his wife.

"Um, well, no." Chester paused. "Maybe. I don't know." He looked down at the floor, and then a slight smile formed at the corners of his mouth. "I guess one," he said, full of hope and thinking about Don Richards.

"Good, because you're going to need at least one." The old man wasn't smiling. "A good one. One you can trust."

"For what?"

"For what we're about to do." Lander went back to his paper.

THESE DAYS

After what felt like a short but good night's sleep, Leland awakened thinking a little about Snoshu and a lot about the bar and the girl. After a good night's sleep, Potter was thinking about breakfast and a pee.

"Hi, girl, how about a little breakfast and a morning walk?" The master spoke directly to the pup. As she was wont, she said nothing but simply cocked her head, which, in Bernese mountain dog speak, spoke volumes. Pretty much regardless of the time of year, early mornings in the mountains were a little chilly, so Leland threw on a US Open sweatshirt over his T-shirt and shorts. He had driven by a park on the way to Jeremy's, so he knew where he was headed. Potter already had her coat on, as well as most of her stuff in the car, so she eagerly leapt into the back of the Wagoneer. For some strange reason, Leland felt the park seemed closer to the house from this direction, and it looked to be even more perfect for a walk than he had hoped. There was a trail, a stream, and a mix of people walking dogs, dogs walking people, and dogless people jogging. Potter wagged her tail, let Leland clip her leash to the collar, and then jumped down from the back of the Jeep.

Walking along at a steady clip, Leland started to tell Potter about the girl he met the night before. Clearly enthralled, the Berner walked a few feet ahead, sniffed the air and then the ground before hunching her body to take a poop. "Thanks for listening," Leland said, pulling a plastic bag from his back pocket. After the cleanup the walk continued, with Leland, this time, keeping his thoughts about the beautiful bartender to himself. He wondered things guys wonder like, is going back tonight too soon? And if it was, when would be the right time to go back to Catcher in the Rye?

Suddenly she was right in front of him, just a few yards away, head-phones in her ears, jogging. She smiled as she passed, and he smiled back, a little hurt because she apparently didn't recognize him. He lowered his head for the next few steps.

"Hey," he heard, and his spirits were immediately uplifted, so he lifted his head and turned around. The dog didn't stop until the lead ran out, but when it did she turned and pranced back to her master and a new human with which to make friends.

"Fancy meeting you here," she said skeptically, continuing to jog in place. Leland wasn't sure if she was going to stop or take off and leave him standing there, hat and leash in hand. Then she stopped and stooped.

"Who's this?" she asked, showing the back of her hand to the Berner. "Oh my God, what a beauty."

"This is Potter," Leland said as he thought, *It works! A gorgeous girl is talking to me because of my dog!* Potter wagged her tail and burrowed her snout between her new found friend's thighs.

"She likes to go between people's legs and get a butt rub," Leland said, not really sure why the dog did it or why he said it.

"Smart girl." She giggled then stood and obliged, letting the Berner happily do her thing. Rubbing the dog's haunches per request, she looked at Leland and smiled.

"Fancy meeting you here," she said again, this time more sincerely.

The sound of that sincerity sent Leland into a reverie. *This kind of shit only happens in movies, books, and dreams,* he thought. *I haven't been able to get her out of my head, and now here she is, and she's a dog person!*

"Hello?" She spoke again. "Did I lose you to another ponytail tale?" She asked, shaking Leland out of mini daydream.

"Sorry," he said, feeling a blush coming on, "I was just marveling at how amazing it is that I was just thinking about you and you show up. I mean, doesn't that stuff only happen in the movies or in dreams?"

She went to her knees again as Potter hit the grass and rolled over on her back, hoping this time for a belly rub.

"You know what else only happens in dreams, books, movies, and TV?" she asked, giving the pup what she wanted. "Nobody ever seems to have to eat or go to the bathroom." She looked at Leland, a bit of a blush showing on her cheeks too, and then she chuckled.

"I mean, come on! Nobody ever has to grab a bite or take a shit!" She stopped and then started. "Wait, did I just say that out loud?" she mused. "Wait, did you just say you were thinking about me?"

Leland marveled at how her mind seemed to work and told her so.

"I marvel at how your mind works."

She stood and shrugged her shoulders. Leland gave the leash a tug and the dog rolled over and stood up, panting, wagging her tail and looking for another pet.

"Yes, I was thinking about you." Leland looked in her eyes and quoted from one of his favorite Jackson Browne songs. "I mean, just look at yourself; what else would I do?"

"Oh God," she groaned.

Oh God, Leland thought, *did I just say that?*

"Did you just feed me a Jackson Browne lyric as a line?" She smiled.

"Why yes, I guess I did." He smiled back. "Wanna walk with us?"

"That would be really nice," she answered, grabbing the dog's leash. "C'mon, girl, let's go." And off they went, with Potter's master close behind. They had walked a few feet when Leland realized that the only name that had been mentioned was the one belonging to the Bernese mountain dog. He stopped. She stopped.

"I'm Leland," he said, "Leland David." He held out his hand.

The dog took her rightful place between the two adults.

"I'm Denny," she said, taking his hand. "Denny King."

"Nice to meet you, Denny," he said, not letting go of her hand. "Is that D-E-M-I, like Demi Moore, only D-E-N-I? he asked.

"Um, yeah," she answered, getting her hand back. "No, not really—actually, not at all. It's D-E-N-N-Y."

"Didn't mean to offend," he said, almost too apologetically.

"No offense taken," she answered back, hoping to assure him. "I told you my dad was a huge J. D. Salinger fan."

"Catcher in the Rye," he remembered out loud.

"Catcher in the Rye," she repeated, "and he named me Holden. She shook her head. "That lasted until I started grade school and the boys began to tease me. I told the kids to call me Denny. For some reason I thought that would be less confusing and more acceptable."

"Did it work?" he asked, hoping the answer was yes but betting it wasn't.

"Nah," she affirmed, "but I liked it, and it's what I've been called ever since."

"I like it," he said, and meant it.

"I don't care," she said, and meant it.

Leland's smile fell off his face, and then one formed on hers.

"Oh wait. Oh shoot," she stammered. "I'm sorry. I didn't mean that to sound so mean. It's just the way it is; it's my name." She looked at Leland. "I'm really happy you like it." And she meant that too.

They walked and talked and talked and walked. They laughed and learned more things about each other and finally found a bench and continued the conversation. The dog lay at their feet during the entire time they sat.

"Why Potter?" she asked, looking at the dog, not Leland.

"Long story short, when she was a puppy, the white fur between her eyes looked like a lightning bolt." Denny looked up at Leland as he continued. "And trying to be clever"—he shrugged—"I named her Harriet Potter." The girl smiled and turned her attention back to the Berner.

"Poor baby," she said, scratching the pup behind her right ear. "Leland?" she said.

"Denny?" he said back.

"I'm famished, *and* I have to go to the bathroom."

THOSE DAYS

"Put them back." The voice was a whisper but familiar to Don Richards. He didn't move a muscle.

"Don't do it. Put them back." Again, a whisper but more aggressive. Richards's hand instinctively went to the front of his pants, where he had just stuffed a pack of White Owl cigarillos. Then he turned his head slowly and came nose to nose with Chester David. Their faces were so close, Richards could see a cluster of blackhead pimples forming at the crease just above the kid's left nostril. He was in a catcher's squat; the smaller boy was bent over with his hands on his knees.

"Put them back," David said again, his breath smelling like bubble gum.

"What?" Richards offered weakly. "Put what back?"

"The cigarettes. In your pants."

"I don't have any cigarettes in my pants," the older boy said defiantly, and for the record correctly. "They're cigars, cigarillos to be exact." He smirked.

"Put them back," Chester David said for the third time, "now."

"Why should I?" the bigger boy countered, suddenly feeling his oats again.

"Because they know you took them."

"Who is *they*?" Richards turned his head from side to side looking past the kid. "There's nobody else in the aisle."

"The Landers know." Chester placed his hand on the bigger boy's shoulder, forcing eye contact again. "Trust me. They know."

Richards held Chester's gaze and knew in his heart the boy was telling the truth. He didn't know how—he had been as sneaky as ever, maybe sneakier, and a handful of minutes ago, he was sure he was walking out of the store with newly pilfered booty stuffed down the front of his Levi 501 jeans. But right this second, because of the conviction of this slightly strange, oddly likeable kid, he was equally certain of exactly the opposite. He simply nodded his head, reached into his pants, pulled out the box of miniature cigars, then stood up, and put them back where he found them.

"OK," he said, without looking at Chester. Then he turned so he could look at the boy, who had also straightened up. "But how did you know they knew?"

Chester considered his companion. Could he call him a friend? He desperately wanted to believe that's what they had become.

"Buy a Coke or a pack of cards" was all he said, and then he turned and walked down the aisle and out the door.

Richards circled back through the store and absentmindedly grabbed a pack of baseball cards and Adams Blackjack chewing gum and approached the counter.

"Will that be it, dear?" old lady Lander asked from behind the cash register.

"Yes, ma'am," Richards answered, reaching into his pocket for a dollar.

"I'm thrilled to see you're giving up smoking," Mrs. Lander said, with a slight smile, freezing Richards with a stare. The way she said it, coupled with the look in her eyes, made the hair on Don Richards's neck stand on end. He shivered slightly. Suddenly and completely unnerved, he left the cards and the gum on the counter, put the buck back in his pocket and turned on his heels, hurrying out the door. Chester was standing next to his bike in the parking lot, waiting.

"What the hell?" Richards asked rhetorically.

"Meet me back here tonight after dinner, around seven," Chester offered as a reply, then he climbed on his bike and pedaled away.

"What the hell?" Richards said again, this time to nobody.

THESE DAYS

The afternoon sex was frantic, fantastic, and, much to Leland's dismay, fast. His head rested on Denny's chest, and he breathlessly spoke into a still-hard nipple.

"I, uh…" He paused. "It's been a while," he said sheepishly. She grabbed him by the hair, which hung just above the base of his neck and gently pulled it back so their eyes could meet.

"Stop" was all she said.

"It's just, I…" He didn't stop. "I can do better."

"I expect you can," she answered and then smiled. "Seriously it was good. A little quick, but good," she added, then let go of his hair and moved her hand much lower on his body.

"It appears you're ready to try again."

THOSE DAYS

"Why did you take the damn cigars when you don't even smoke?" Lander spoke the rhetorical question as he, Chester, Mrs. Lander, and Richards sat around the couple's kitchen table. The thief rubbed his left hand over the plastic red-and-white-checkered tablecloth and shrugged his shoulders. He had come back at seven as instructed, met Chester, who ushered him into the store and through the back door that led to the Landers' living quarters. Warm, homemade chocolate chip cookies and ice-cold milk waited. As did questions, lots and lots of questions, asked by the old man. More questions than answers as it turned out, because more often than not, Richards struggled with an explanation.

"I don't know." Richards stammered out the beginnings of a reply to Lander's most recent query, shrugged his ample shoulders again, and then added, "For fun?" It came out in the form of an uncertainty.

"Is it?" Lander asked, certain he knew the answer.

"Is it what?" Richards responded.

"Fun. Is taking something that isn't yours for no reason fun?" The inquisitor stared at his mark. Richards took a moment to consider that.

"I don't know," he said, shaking his head, "I guess." Lander stared but said nothing. Richards shifted slightly, gave Chester a quick look,

97

then dropped his eyes to the tabletop, and continued. "It's exciting." He looked up at Lander with a smile, thinking he had unlocked the secret. Unmoved, Lander continued to look at the young man. Richards, so confident a second ago, now wondered if there was a better word. "It's more than the excitement. It's…it's…" Try as he might, the word or words just didn't come out.

"Exhilarating?" The voice was Mrs. Lander, and it came from behind the open refrigerator door.

When did she get up from the table? Richards wondered to himself, and then said out loud, "Yeah, exhilarating, that's exactly what it is." He smiled, but then the smile faded. "At least at first," he added, "but that feeling goes away pretty quickly." He looked at the old man. "It's actually…" The boy paused again, wishing silently he had a better command of the words.

"Dispiriting?" The woman again, this time standing right next to him, placing a small but surprisingly strong hand on his shoulder. "Joyless?"

"I guess," Richards replied, looking a little sadly at Mrs. Lander.

"You have to get over that!" The old man raised his voice and lowered his fist onto the table. Richards jumped in his seat, and Chester laughed out loud, letting loose a chunk or two of half-chewed cookie from his mouth.

"You two friends?" Another question from Lander to Richards, asked as his right index finger waggled between the two boys.

"Me and him?" Richards turned a thumb in Chester's direction.

"No, you and my bride! Of course, you and him." Lander shook his head and turned his own thumb toward the younger boy. Richards regarded the kid but answered in seconds. "Yeah. We're friends." Mentally Chester breathed a sigh of relief, and then he smiled.

"Good," Lander said, snatching a cookie. He looked at Richards, then longer at Chester, forcing the older boy to follow his gaze. "Cuz this kid here could snatch the sleep from a napping infant, and the baby would be no wiser for it. He can take his time, your time, and my time, all at the same time, but he's gonna need friends to pull off the heists that I have planned." For the second time in seconds, Chester smiled.

"Friends?" Richards asked the question this time.

"Yep" was the simple first response. Then the older gentleman elucidated. "Me, Evelyn"—at the sound of her name, the woman instinctively raised her hand—"and now you." Lander pointed his crooked-at-the-tip left index finger at Richards. "We're going to do some things, and we are not going to do other things," Lander looked through Richards and picked up another cookie. "We're gonna take things from people and places. That's what we're *gonna* do!" He took a bite of cookie and chewed slowly. Richards looked at Chester, who acknowledged the look with a small nod, and then looked at Lander who had finished chewing. "What we are *not* gonna do is physically hurt anybody." Lander looked around the room, but he wasn't finished. "And we aren't going to feel *dispirited* about it when we're done." His eyes met Don Richards's one more time. "You in?"

And that was the evening's last question.

THESE DAYS

The rest of the day/evening/night was a blur. They talked, they laughed, they ate, they drank, and yes, they both went to the bathroom. Leland and Denny only left her apartment to take the dog out so she could go to the bathroom too. The girl-of-his-dreams' place was a collection of rooms above the Catcher in the Rye bar. It was well appointed, well kept, and tasteful with enchanting touches like an elephant head sculpture above the toilet in the bathroom and a two-foot-tall hourglass replete with white sand on a sofa table. Leland loved the place and immediately felt right at home. So did Potter, who took it upon herself to plop down on what appeared to be a very expensive Persian rug in the middle of the living room.

"Is she OK there?" he had asked.

"She's OK anywhere she wants to be," Denny had replied, and Leland had slipped a little deeper down the rabbit hole.

They never turned on the TV, did turn on, and up, the radio and danced a slow dance around the dog to Pat Green's *Dixie Lullaby*. They ended up in Denny's bed fulfilled, enthralled, and exhausted, or at least Leland was. Denny must have been as well. The three of them had taken another long dog walk, and two of the three enjoyed a first dinner together. Then she fell asleep almost immediately after brushing her teeth and changing into something more comfortable: full-length pajamas. Leland, while tired, found no sleep. Every time he closed his eyes, he relived the hours that had just passed and enjoyed the experience over again. He lay on his side, head propped up by his right arm, and watched Denny sleep. Her breathing was slow and steady. On the floor, on her back, on Denny's side of the bed, lay the dog, snoring. He looked at his main companion for the last eighteen months and felt something, but what? It wasn't anger, jealousy, or envy, no way. He realized it was actually empathy, one magnificent creature wanting to be as close as possible to another magnificent creature. Leland smiled. He couldn't blame the dog for that. Who could? He shifted from his side to flat on his back and closed his eyes again. He tried again to summon sleep, but it proved as dogged as ever in its determination to keep him conscious. He was still too excited to sleep, too aroused, too cognizant of his surroundings, fully aware of his feelings but unsettled about what they meant and what, if anything, he could, should, and would do about them.

He adjusted his position once again and stared at the woman sleeping next to him. Beautiful, funny, interesting, and smart, no doubt. Was she also too good to be true? He wondered. The word smitten wormed its way into his jumbled brain and stayed there, neon green, in a sea of other images, thoughts, and ideas. He smiled and slowly, silently slid off the mattress, making every effort to not wake either girl, the person or the pup. Mission accomplished, he tiptoed around the bed and turned to take one last look at the two of them, one on her stomach, the other paws and belly up on her back. Both dead to the world. He couldn't help but wonder what in the world was going on. From the moment he awakened (how many days ago was that?), he had managed to meet a girl, find Don Richards, and start the winding, wistful process of figuring out answers to the questions about his father. What if he had gone left instead of right on that street the other night? What if he had decided *not* to read the paper on the porch? He would have never crossed paths with this amazing woman or gathered the information that pointed him in the direction of his long-lost "uncle." But he did and he did, so now what?

He wandered through the rooms, realizing the apartment was bigger than he had first realized. He thought again how nice it was, with rooms that could be photographed and then shared with the world in any of a dozen magazines or catalogues from stores, shops, and retailers that he had seen over the years. But as hard as he looked, he failed to find anything personal, something clearly hers, on any of the walls, shelves, or nooks. There were candles and vases full of realistic-looking but fake flowers, meticulously placed on tables in many of the rooms. He noticed a painting or two on the wall and several framed photographs of familiar places, including the Acropolis, Aspen, and Angel Falls, but Denny wasn't in any of them. A strange feeling that the only place Denny could be found was in the adjacent bedroom washed over him. It struck him as more than a little odd that there was nothing that said her name, no photo with her in the middle of a group of smiling friends or memento that looked oddly out of place from some bustling bazaar purchased in some nearby or faraway town. The introspection lasted seconds, and as he took a second look around the place, he came to the conclusion that it all said Denny, happily announcing her presence everywhere he turned. Then his eyes settled on a stand-alone row of shelves in a far corner of the main living area. It was filled with books.

There appeared to be no rhyme or reason how or why the tomes were arranged on the shelves. Fiction stood shoulder to shoulder with nonfiction, separated occasionally by a work of poetry, a dictionary, or the King James Bible. He also noticed a Koran, a decades old *Guinness Book of World Records*, and an *Encyclopedia Britannica*, Volume 8, showing within its pages information on everything from "EDWA to EXHAUT," according to the weathered, leather spine. He saw volumes penned by some of his favorite authors—Nelson DeMille, Stuart Woods, Terry Pratchett, John Feinstein, and Michael Connelly. In addition to those, there was *Catch-22*, *The Adventures of Huckleberry Finn*, *To Kill a Mockingbird*, and *One Flew over the Cuckoo's Nest*. A smile came to his face when he saw J. D. Salinger's most famous work, *Catcher in the Rye*, next to another not-quite-as-famous Salinger book, *Franny and Zooey*, and guessed they were either gifts given by or homages to her father. For a second, perhaps longer, he thought about pulling one off the shelf to see if it was personally inscribed by her late dad, but he decided, in the next second, against it. There was also Irving and Orwell, Puzo and Tolkien. His eye glanced over *A Little Prince, The Lion, The Witch and The Wardrobe, The Very Hungry Caterpillar,* and *Where the Wild Things Are.* Memories came flooding back, and mystery inched its way into his conscious mind.

"Who is this girl?" he thought out loud, and then his line of sight dropped to a shelf that harbored a series of books that stopped him short and produced a sharp intake of breath. "I think that was my first gasp," he muttered as he read. The tome that seemed so oddly out of place was *The Human Comedy*, a multivolume collection of novels and stories by the long-dead French philosopher, Honore de Balzac.

"Who the fuck has Balzac on their bookshelf?" he said, a little louder than he wanted to.

"Clearly I do," Denny said from the doorway. Potter, bushy tail propellering in delight, was by her side.

THOSE DAYS

"**D**o we have a nickname?" Richards put the car in park and stared out the front windshield.

"What?" Leland looked up from the book that lay open on his lap.

"Do we have a nickname, an alias? You know, like the Hole in the Wall Gang or the Wild Bunch? Come on; you know what I'm talking about, a nom de plume," he uttered, the last three syllables with a horribly affected French accent. Chester looked at his best friend as if he had never seen him before in his life. Then he shook his head.

"You mean a nom de guerre, and no, we don't."

"Nom de what?" It was times like this that Don Richards thought he wanted to punch his smart-aleck buddy in the nose, but he knew better, and the thought, like it always did, passed quickly. "What's the difference?" he asked instead.

"A nom de plume is French for pen name, specifically something a writer would use, and a nom de guerre means an assumed name. It was used during wartime as a code name or nickname for spies and guys like that."

"Wow, learn something new every day." Richards smiled.

"Easier for you than me," Chester answered, under his breath. This time Richards didn't think twice about the punch, landing one square on the smaller kid's left bicep. The smile, however, stayed on his face.

"Well, all I'm saying is, I think we need a nickname." Richards got in the last word as they both got out of the car and headed for the movie theatre.

"What's this movie about?" Don asked Chester, who was still rubbing his left arm.

"Good and evil," Chester answered.

"Well, that narrows it down," Richards said, looking at the marquee. "Judy Garland in *The Wizard of Oz*," he read out loud. "Is there magic involved?"

"What?" Chester looked at his friend.

"Magic, you know, making things appear and disappear. Isn't that what wizards do?"

"I guess it is" was Chester's response. "I don't know. What I do know is the star, Judy Garland, used to sing at the casino where my dad worked." His friend whistled.

"Did you ever see her sing?"

"Once," Chester remembered his father had actually kept a promise. "But her name was Frances Gumm."

"See, we need an alias," Richards said proudly.

"Chester?" A vaguely familiar voice came from someone a few folks behind the boys in line. Chester turned at the sound of his name.

"Coach Carmichael?" He recognized his old coach and martial-arts teacher instantly. So did Don Richards who had also turned.

"Richards," the coach said, acknowledging the other young man.

"Coach." Richards nodded back. Eddie Carmichael turned his attention back to Chester. *Growing up into quite an impressive-looking young man,* he thought.

"*The Wizard of Oz?*" he asked skeptically. Chester raised both hands in mock surrender. They were, after all, the youngest people in line.

"The power of love, kindness, and acceptance over cruelty, hate, and fear," he answered.

"Indeed." The coach smiled back. "Enjoy."

Chester and Richards turned back toward the ticket booth. A ten-foot space had opened up since the conversation began. They were now next in line.

"What the heck was that all about?" Richards asked his pal.

"Lessons learned, I guess" was Chester David's reply. "Two please," he said to the girl in the booth.

"My treat," Richards interjected, and slid some bills through the gap in the window.

They had been doing all sorts of jobs, cashing in on what old man Lander called "wrongs that needed righting," like modern-day Robin Hoods, Chester thought, except for the fact that they didn't give their ill-gotten gains to the poor; they kept them. They even "collected" more than ten thousand dollars from the very full, very easy-to-crack safe of one Mike "Big Mikey" Moran, Marty's father. According to Lander, Big Mikey was a ham-fisted, hard-assed union boss who had a habit of conning his constituents out of extra dues that the people he represented neither actually owed or, in some cases, could afford to pay. Like his son, Mike Moran was a bully, and he was a lot better at it than his fat kid.

Few people liked him, and none liked him less than Mr. Lander, who cringed every time the older Moran entered the store. Maybe because each visit ended with the self-professed "tough guy" leaving with a six-pack under one arm, a fistful of Slim Jims in one hand, and a "put it on my tab" out of his fat-lipped mouth as he was backing out the door; to add insult to injury, that injustice was almost always followed by another, more egregious one. A salute with his free hand and a smirk on his unshaven face that shouted, "What are you gonna do about it, old man?" The "old man" was well versed and well connected enough to know he had several options at his disposal, including good old-fashioned East Coast mob justice. But thanks to careful planning and the nimble fingers of Chester David, Emmett Lander exacted his subtler, more fulfilling form of revenge.

THESE DAYS

"It's so weird," he started to say, "I have almost all of these books at home." He gestured to the bookcase, but kept his eyes on Denny. "Of course they aren't quite as neatly displayed." The dog at the girl's side continued to wag her bushy tail.

"Even Balzac?" she said, tilting her head—the girl, that is, not the dog.

"Even Balzac," he answered. "My pop had 'em, and I guess his pop, my grandpa, before that."

"Wow," she said, starting to walk his way. The dog followed. "You said *had* them." She reached for and grabbed his hand. He held on tight, knowing what was coming next. "Am I correct to assume by your use of the past tense that your dad has passed away?"

"You are," he answered flatly. "My mom too." She looked at him more closely, scrutinizing his face. He didn't appear sad, and she wasn't sure if that bothered her. She cried for weeks after her father died and still cried at random times now and again.

"Jesus" was all she said.

"Car wreck took my dad," he said. "Food got my mom." Despite best efforts, she couldn't contain the guffaw that exploded from her lips. The sound made him smile too.

"I'm sorry," she said about the outburst, "what did you say?"

"Food," he repeated. "She choked on a shrimp at her favorite restaurant." He stopped but only for a second or maybe two. "Seems no one in the place knew the Heimlich maneuver."

"I'm so sorry," she said.

"Thanks. It's OK," he said in all sincerity. "We weren't very close when she died."

"Still," she countered, "she *was* your mother."

"Yes, she was."

"Besides the Balzac, what did your dad leave behind?" she wondered, hoping to change the subject. "And don't tell me a bar."

"Ha!" It was his turn to blurt out a laugh. "Wouldn't that be an amazing coincidence? Nope, not a bar, but he did leave a house, a shitload of money, and, as I've recently discovered, more questions than answers." He looked away from her and down at the Berner, who was staring at her new best friend and hoping for some more attention.

"What do you mean by that?" Denny absentmindedly rubbed the dog's head. Leland said nothing for several seconds, trying to decide the best way to broach what he wanted to say next. Then he lifted his head and looked into her bright, blue eyes.

"If it's OK with you, I'd really rather show you than tell you." Still holding hands, he squeezed hers a little tighter. "But it means a trip west with me." He looked down at the dog again. "And her."

"I'll go pack a bag" was Denny's answer.

THOSE DAYS

Chester noticed something was different the second he walked through the side door of the Landers' house; Richards noticed a full plate of still-warm chocolate chip cookies in the center of the kitchen table. On most occasions when the boys, now young men, met with the Landers, the old man sat in the same chair, at that same kitchen table, purposefully—a man with some kind of a plan firmly in his mind. It could be a theft, a teaching moment, or an opportunity to do a little "team building." But on this occasion, old man Lander's usual chair was empty. Mrs. Lander was at the oven, back to the boys, either putting in or taking out more baked goods. The kitchen smelled amazing. Chester noticed a New Jersey newspaper on the table.

"TROUBLED TEEN TAKES OWN LIFE" was the headline that attracted his attention. Beneath it was the story of a boy in Patterson, New Jersey, named Conner Suarez. The words on the page screamed an all-too-familiar story. Chester read that Conner dreamed of dancing for the American Ballet Theatre instead of becoming a power forward for the New York Knicks, and he paid the price for that. According to an aunt, he had been continually and mercilessly picked on, harassed, and belittled by a physically overzealous, mentally underdeveloped bully at his school. Reading the newsprint rekindled a rage in Chester, one that he'd thought he had contained, controlled.

Suddenly he could smell Marty Moran's breath in his nostrils and feel the spittle on his flesh. It made his skin crawl. He wanted to punch a hole in the wall, but at that moment, reading about a tormented kindred spirit thousands of miles away, he realized it might be less painful and more compassionate to punch a hole in an ethos. He read on, hoping to find more information than just a relative's last name. What he found instead broke off a little piece of his heart. Conner Suarez decided he was tired of the battle, so he jumped off one of the bridges that connected New Jersey to New York. "Jesus," he whispered, and then thought about Coach Carmichael, Don Richards, Evelyn and Emmet Lander, and where he might be without them. He would help someone else.

"Would you like a cookie?" Mrs. Lander put her hand on his left shoulder.

"Where's the boss man?" Chester reached his right hand across his chest to find the top of hers.

"Can I have a cookie?" Richards asked, right hand already reaching for the goodies on the plate.

"Of course," Mrs. Lander answered the second boy.

"In here." From his favorite leather recliner in the living room, Mr. Lander answered the first.

Chester had been in that room a couple of times, but Richards never had. They both headed that way, Chester in the lead. Before they went through the entryway, Chester stopped, turned, and put a hand on his best friend's shoulder.

"Why don't you put the cookies back." He whispered it as a statement, not a question.

"Why?" Richards whispered back. "What's going on?"

"Not sure." Chester looked back over his shoulder toward the living room and then back at his friend. "Just put the cookies back. No food in the living room." And he smiled almost like he knew what was coming next. Richards looked disappointed, but before he could turn disappointment into defiance, Mrs. Lander spoke.

"No food in the living room, dear," she called, back at her spot near the oven, eyes in the back of her head, and ears everywhere. Richards shook his head and returned the cookies, and then the two of them headed into the meeting. Chester didn't hesitate, but he did worry just a little, wracking his brain, reliving the last few heists. Were they noticed? Did they leave behind a clue that would lead the police, or the aggrieved, to either him or Lander? He didn't come up with anything, couldn't think of being at all careless. As far as he could recall, in those few steps between the kitchen chair on which Lander usually sat and the Barcalounger in which he now reclined, everything had gone off without a hitch. *But you never know* was the last thing Chester thought before Lander spoke.

"Come on in, fellas," he said. "Have a seat." He pointed, with a pistol in his hand, to a leather couch. Chester froze. Richards, not paying attention, walked right into his back.

"What the!" he groaned. He looked at Chester, annoyed, and then at Lander. "Jesus Christ!"

Lander's head turned toward the two young men, one stoic, one clearly scared to death. That slight motion meant the barrel was now pointed directly at the visitors. He cocked his head, not the handgun. Chester stoically looked at Lander. Richards threw up his hands and fell to his knees.

"What did we do?" he screeched. "Please don't shoot us!"

Chester, eyes still on Lander, reached down with his left hand and lifted Richards to his feet. "Relax, Don," he said in a steady, reassuring voice. "He's not going to shoot anybody, especially us."

"What?" Lander blurted, eyes now focused on his protégé. "Why in the hell would I shoot you?" he asked, but both boys noticed the gun was still pointed in their direction. Richards pointed a shaking left index finger at it. Lander's eyes followed the motion and landed on the handgun. He let out a laugh.

"Oh shit! This?" The laugh became a statement and then a question. "Holding it helps me think," he said as an explanation. "Geez, it isn't even loaded." He tossed the weapon at Richards, who continued to stand and point, mouth agape. Chester caught the gun with his left hand before it hit Richards square in the face.

"C'mon, sit down." The old man motioned toward the couch again, this time without the pistol. "We have something important to discuss."

THESE DAYS

The next several hours seemed to pass in a flash. Leland tried but couldn't remember anything that happened between "I'll pack a bag" and the very moment in which he now found himself: driving, Denny sitting on the passenger side of the Jeep Wagoneer bench front seat. Their luggage was packed and on the backseat. Had he gone back to Jeremy's and retrieved his stuff? He must have because it was sitting right there being watched over by a yawning Bernese mountain dog.

He stole another glance at the girl to his right. *Had she gotten more beautiful? Was that even possible?* Yes, she had, he decided, and then he wondered again how the hell the stars had aligned in such a way that brought her not only into his life but into his head and heart. *It feels like a dream,* he thought.

"It is." Her words smashed through his reverie like an out-of-control eighteen-wheeler that had just exhausted its last bit of breaks with plenty of downhill left to go. For a brief, fleeting, fucked-up moment, he felt a wave of nausea overtake him.

"It is?" he blurted out.

"Yes, it is," she reiterated, but in very undreamlike fashion. Instead of disappearing before his very eyes, she looked right at him, through him, and continued. "It is extremely rude to stare." She gave him a smile, then added, "And dangerous when you are behind the wheel."

He breathed a sigh of relief. Did she notice?

"I have an idea," she said, appearing not to have. "You drive; I'll look at the scenery."

"No fair," he protested lamely, regaining his bearings. "It's so easy on the eyes."

She smiled again, this time looking out the window instead of in the car. "You drive; I'll look," she repeated.

He drove.

THOSE DAYS

The plan that Lander laid out, while thinking with a gun in his hand, involved a car ride across the border into Mexico. Just Chester and Richards. They took shifts: one driving, one resting, or occasionally sleeping until they reached where the United States of America ended and the United States of Mexico began. Traffic was light at the dimly lit border crossing when Chester, at the wheel, arrived. He noticed the three cars in front of theirs moving smoothly.

"Get the papers out." He spoke to and punched Richards on the shoulder at the same time. At either the sound of Chester's voice or the force of the punch, Richards opened his eyes.

"Huh?" he half said, half grunted.

"The papers," Chester repeated, "our IDs. Get them out of the glove compartment."

Richards vigorously shook his head back and forth to exorcise the remaining cobwebs that had settled thanks to a fitful, sitting-up sleep. He opened the tiny door.

"Got 'em," he said as Chester pulled up alongside the guard and rolled down the driver's side window.

"Evening, gentlemen," the uniformed officer said, shining his flashlight into the car to get a better look as to exactly who and what was inside.

"I think it's actually good morning," Chester answered with a smile, a fake yawn, and a check of his watch.

"You're absolutely right," replied the guard with a smile of his own. "What brings you two fellas this way?"

"My friend here is thinking about getting hitched." Chester casually pointed his right thumb at Richards in the passenger seat. "And I feel it's my job, as a friend, to help him get educated on some of the more essential elements of a successful marriage." Then he conspiratorially added, "If you know what I mean," for good measure.

In the passenger seat, Richards shook his head for the second time in five minutes.

"So you've been here before?" The guard dropped the smile.

"I have," Chester said, looking past the flashlight at the man holding it. What seemed to Richards like an uncomfortable silence followed; then the guard burst out laughing.

"Then you know not to drink the water," he said, and waved them through, never looking at the identification Richards still held in his hands.

That was supposed to be the hard part, at least according to Lander, Chester thought as he drove along the mostly deserted streets toward the destination. The National Museum of Anthropology was an easy target, "like taking candy from a bambino," Lander had said, awkwardly mixing languages in his study. Nobody in the building knew the extent of the value of what was housed there, or if they knew, Lander had added, apparently they didn't care, because the museum was frequently deserted and almost always unguarded.

"Do you ever wonder how or why the old man comes up with all these schemes?" It was Richards asking the same question Chester David had asked himself on a number of occasions.

"I never really thought about it," Chester lied. "I just know so far he's batting a thousand, and we're getting rich because of it."

"I guess that's true," Richards said as he opened the glove compartment again. He put back the identification papers and pulled out another sheet—the list of relics he and Chester were supposed to remove from the museum. "But up until now, the jobs were closer to home. Why is this one in Mexico?"

"Why not?" Chester answered his friend matter-of-factly. "Maybe those jobs were tests. Maybe Lander was seeing how good we were or whether or not we could be trusted before giving us something really big."

"You think this is really big?" Richards's eyes looked up and down the paper. "I mean, what is all this stuff? There must be a hundred things here."

"A hundred and forty," Chester responded, having memorized the list, "and they are all at least four hundred years old."

Richards shook his head and continued to look at the list, appearing not to have heard. "I mean, what the heck does the old man want with an obscene monkey?"

Chester laughed out loud and then looked at his best friend. "Obsidian."

"What?" Richards looked up from the sheet of paper and over at Chester.

"It's obsidian, not obscene."

"I guess I read that wrong." They both laughed.

THESE DAYS

Leland continued to drive, REO Speedwagon playing softly through the speakers, thanks to the eight-track player. The dog and Denny slept. He had kept the 1975 Jeep Grand Wagoneer, with its AMC 360 engine and Pioneer TP-6000 eight-track player, in pristine shape. He kept the music maker, simply because he thought it was cool. Luckily, he found a shop near his house that capitalized on the revival of eight-track cassettes, and the owner, Steve, was constantly on the lookout for the bands Leland liked. Over the years he had been offered as much as $50,000 for the car but had never even entertained a passing interest in selling it. It had belonged to his dad. In many ways Leland felt it still did.

Times he spent in introspection were rare, but he smiled to himself as he thought they seemed less rare lately. This was one of those times.

"When I said that I loved you, I meant that I loved you forever," Kevin Cronin crooned.

"Forever," Leland said under his breath and shook his head. "Love songs," he added, with a tiny measure of disdain. He thought about a singer/songwriter he had befriended, who, after Leland had commented on why one particular ballad was his favorite, told him to "get your dick out of your heart. That song sucks." Then he chuckled, slapped Leland on the back, and bought another round.

"What were you thinking about?" It was Denny.

"Hey there," he said, reaching for her hand and realizing he was already holding it. "How long have you been awake?"

"What difference does *that* make?" she answered his question with her own. "What were you thinking about?" she asked again.

He paused and then answered, "Just wondering when it happens."

"When *what* happens?"

Another pause. "When is the moment that the people you *know* become the people you *knew*?" He turned his head to look at her. She looked straight ahead.

"Every second of every day" was her answer.

THOSE DAYS

"Something's not right," Chester thought, then said out loud as he made a left turn, preparing to circle the museum for the second time. Richards sat up a little taller in the passenger seat and looked out the windshield.

"What do you mean?" he asked, something that sounded, to Chester, like concern in his voice.

"Not a huge thing," he said, hoping to reassure himself and his friend. "It just doesn't look or feel right."

"What do you mean?" Richards repeated his query in an entirely different tone of voice, a tone that made it an entirely different question.

"Take a look at the street lamps for one thing." Chester pointed, and Richards looked up.

"What about them?"

"Too bright" was Chester's answer. After a just-longer-than-brief pause, he elaborated. "Mr. Lander said this would be a piece of cake, nobody around, no way we'd be noticed."

"But there are cars parked up and down the street," Richards added, suddenly observant.

"Under several, very bright, street lamps," Chester said, finishing the thought. "And look left." Chester made an effort not to point, looking straight ahead. Richards turned his head and looked past the driver. "Mexican cops," he almost gasped.

Two police cars were parked, parallel to each other and facing opposite directions, allowing the two officers to speak face-to-face.

"We're out of here." Chester drove down the street three blocks and turned right.

Fifteen minutes later they were seated in a booth at a restaurant; each staring at his own cup of coffee.

"What was that all about?" Richards leaned in and whispered the question. They were the first words he had spoken since seeing the police cars.

"Not sure." Chester stirred a little more milk into the coffee he wasn't drinking.

"Do you think Lander set us up?"

Chester stopped stirring and looked up at his companion, anger in his eyes.

"How did your brain go *there*?" he blurted. "Is that honestly what you've been thinking for the last half hour?"

"You can't tell me the same thought didn't cross your mind," Richards said defensively.

"Yes. I can," Chester shot back.

"OK." Richards retreated slightly. "What then?" he half asked, half thought.

"Shhhh," was the response as Chester put his right index finger to his lips. "Listen," he ordered.

Two pretty Mexican women, maybe twenty years old, were in an adjacent booth talking excitedly.

Richards slid over on his bench seat, closer to the girls, and strained to hear better. He could now catch every word and was pleased with himself that he actually understood a few. He had stopped thinking he retained anything from high-school Spanish class. Chester didn't move but listened intently, clearly understanding every word. Seconds ticked by as the girls' conversation became more animated.

"Did she just say something's happening on Christmas Eve?" Richards whispered proudly. Chester put his entire right hand up, palm facing Richards this time, to request silence. His eyes betrayed a look that had turned from anger to admiration for his best friend. The girls finished their chat with giggles.

"I didn't know you could *hablar español.*"

"*Un poco,*" Richards replied, holding up his right hand, index finger and thumb about an inch apart. His smile was from ear to ear.

"Let's go home," Chester said suddenly. He dropped some money on the table and got up. Richards followed, leaving a five-dollar bill and both cups of coffee unsipped.

The last part of Lander's plan had Chester and Don returning to the United States through a specific lane at the border, and that's what Chester did. Even though one lane was clear, they waited in the appointed lane behind a red Ford Fairlane. Once cleared, the red Ford accelerated, leaving the lane open for Chester to slowly approach. He waited until he had come to a complete stop before rolling down the driver's side window. Once down, he looked up at the border security guard. He opened his mouth but could find no words because smiling down at him, eyes under the brim of a US Customs Office hat, was Emmett Lander.

"How did it go, son?" the old man asked.

"It didn't," Chester answered straight-faced. Lander's smile was gone in an instant.

"What do you mean *it didn't?*" he asked, and Chester noticed, for the first time since the night he was caught red-handed in the general store, a hint of menace in Emmett Lander's eyes.

"It didn't go because it didn't look or feel right." Chester stood his ground, mustering up, in the answer, as much of his own menace as he could.

"There were Mexican cops and streetlights," Richards blurted out.

"Hush!" Chester scolded his friend with a word and then addressed his mentor again. "You're just going to have to trust me on this one." He turned his head and stared at the road ahead, the road that led home.

"We'll meet back at the house on Monday and sort this out." Lander's tone seemed to have softened.

Chester nodded, almost imperceptibly, and drove away. When the next car in the queue pulled up, the booth was empty. The crossing guard was gone.

THESE DAYS

"Which one?" she asked, having found two eight-track cassettes she apparently wanted to hear after, or instead of, REO Speedwagon's *Hi Infidelity*.

"Can I look?" he asked, smiling inside and out. She smiled too.

"Just for a second," she answered.

In her left hand, she held the Eagles' *Hotel California,* and in her right was a copy of *Tea for the Tillerman,* by Cat Stevens.

"Don't care." He chose not to choose despite the fact that the Eagles would have been his choice. In reality he was more than a little surprised that he still had *Tea for the Tillerman* in his collection. Once upon a time, he remembered he also owned *Teaser and the Firecat and Catch Bull at Four* in addition to *Tillerman.* But when Stevens famously converted to Islam, changed his name to Yusef, auctioned off all his guitars, and left his music career and—Leland felt—his fans in the dust, he made the decision to do the same to the singer who was once Cat. He thought he had tossed all those eight-tracks.

I really do like the song "Father and Son," Leland thought, coming up with what must have been the reason for keeping this one eight-track cassette while shit-canning the rest.

"Let's listen to the Eagles," he heard her say as if she had read his mind. "I love 'New Kid in Town.'"

"Me too."

THOSE DAYS

They were back in the room in which the Mexican museum caper was first revealed to Chester and Don Richards. No gun this time. Instead Emmett Lander held a crystal glass, containing what he referred to as "three fingers" of Pappy Van Winkle bourbon. He had also offered similar drinks to the two young men, and both accepted, one gladly, the other a bit more reluctantly. Leland didn't immediately take to the amber liquid and the slight burn it produced in his throat, while Richards swirled it, sniffed it, and then sipped it like a pro.

It was Tuesday, not Monday, as Lander first suggested, giving everyone in the room an extra day to think about what they wanted to say. Two of the three, as usual, did most the talking.

"There were actual, honest-to-God *policemen* in the area?" Lander seemed to stare right through Chester.

"Two, in cars, like I said," Chester answered.

"But what spooked you was the brightness of the street lamps?" Lander focused, now staring right at Chester, waiting for the answer.

"It all troubled me, sir." He spoke with sincere reverence. "The cops, the cars on the street, and, yes, the brightness of the street lamps." He paused and raised the glass to his lips but didn't sip. "It was supposed to be a piece of cake, a 'walk in the park' was how I remember you put it, but it wasn't. If anybody, including those two cops, just happened to be watching, they would have had no problem identifying us or our car." He stopped, lifted the glass again, and took a sip, hoping this one would go down more smoothly than the last. It didn't. "I just knew in my heart *and* my head that the best thing to do was to pull the plug."

"Smart boy." Lander was looking at Richards now. "Very smart boy."

"So what do we do now?" Richards spoke for the first time, feeling he had been called upon to do so.

Lander's mouth formed a thin, small smile. "What you do now is listen to a story."

"Before you start"—Richards dared to interrupt—"can I have three more fingers of that Poppy?" he asked, holding out his glass.

"It's Pappy, and sure," Lander said, rising from his chair and pouring from the monogrammed decanter. "Now sit back and shut up." Don Richards did both.

"I'm not from around here," Lander started, after refilling his own glass.

No kidding, thought Chester sarcastically.

"No *kidding*?" Richards said, genuinely surprised and forgetting the second part of Lander's instructions. Both Lander and Chester turned to look at the third member of the group. Chester's mouth was agape, Lander's now a wicked grin.

"No kidding," Lander said as he and Richards shook their heads for completely different reasons. Richards took a healthy sip of his whiskey. Lander looked away from the one boy and set his gaze on the other. Then he told his story.

"When I was a kid growing up in New Jersey, my dad was a tough guy, my uncles were tough guys, and so I thought I was a tough guy," he started. What followed was a tale of adventure featuring real-life people who sounded more like fictional characters. Characters, most of whom had nicknames that included The Gent, Jimmy "The Gimp," Icepick, and Good-Lookin' Sal. There was a big guy named Midget and a little one who went by Big G. It was filled with stories about break-ins, bribery, broads, betrayal, and brotherhood. Both Chester and Richards sat rapt, neither touching their drinks since the moment Lander had started.

"Everything worked; nobody could stop us," Lander said, looking first at Chester and then out the window. "Until it didn't...and they did." The last part seemed to hang for an extra second in the air, as if the words were somehow slightly less heavy than the ones that had come before. They finally floated away as the protégé and his friend stared hungrily at Lander, hoping there was more. Sensing the anticipation and owning it, Lander waited an extra breath or two before he gave them what they were longing for—more.

"Lucky for me there was a girl." As if on cue, Mrs. Lander entered the room and allowed herself a slight smile of her own. Chester thought she looked like she knew the whole story, which, of course, she did. The slight yet strong woman stood by her man and put her right hand on her husband's right shoulder. Lander didn't hesitate reaching across his chest with his left hand to pat it lovingly. He looked at his wife and smiled before turning back to his audience.

"Refill?" he asked both with one question, knowing full well neither had touched a drop since the story had started more than an hour ago. Chester slowly shook his head, while Richards took a big swig of bourbon and then nodded, holding his glass out for more. Lander refilled that glass and his own.

"I owe everything to the girl," he said, referring to yet not looking at his wife. "Someone once said, 'We are all just chemicals wrapped up in miracles,' and that was what she was to me, a miracle." The girl, he would go on to explain, was Evelyn Josephina "Jo" Messina, now Lander. She was the daughter of a New Jersey mob boss who wanted her life to be one of a little less crime but an equal amount of comfort to his own. He saw a young, eager Emiliano Lassiter, now Emmett Lander, as a way to accomplish that.

Joseph "Big Nose Joe" Messina ran the organization with a ruthless iron fist. He was mirthless and merciless when it came to his men *and* his enemies but a giant teddy bear when it came to his daughter.

He had earned his nickname not because of the size of his proboscis, which in reality was quite petite, almost delicate, but because he had the much valued ability to sniff out rats, snitches, and undercover cops. While he exhibited a great deal of imagination in dishing out punishment, he showed a complete lack of it when it came to naming his first and, as it turned out, only offspring, who he lovingly christened Evelyn Josephina.

Messina was quite fond of the young lad, liked his pluck, his smarts, and his ability to get every job he was asked to do done without any drama. The "boss" had no issue with the interest Emiliano showed when it came to his daughter, nor the mutual feelings she couldn't conceal showing back. He even entertained the thought of keeping both kids around, but ultimately decided that would put his only daughter in too much peril. New gangs, more aggressive and ruthless, were popping up all over New York and New Jersey, and the wannabe gangsters indicated no willingness to respect the ways of the world or the families that had run that world for as long as Big Nose Joe could remember. So he sacrificed seeing his daughter every day to set her and young Lassiter up out west. Before they left, young Emiliano asked the mob boss for his blessing to marry the beautiful Josephina. He received it without hesitation.

"Change your name and get yourself a respectable job." Lander told the boys what his future father-in-law had said in a perfect "Big Nose Joe Messina New Jersey" accent. "Become a pillar of the community. Don't worry; we'll be here when we need you." Everybody in the room, including Jo Lander, laughed at that one.

"So we did, and they were," Lander said, his voice his own again. He took a long slug from his glass of whiskey.

With seed money from his father-in-law, Lander bought the tiny store and the house that enveloped it. Then he joined the Rotary Club, the Kiwanis, and even one year ran for and was elected to serve on the city council. All the while coded messages would arrive in the form of family recipes, detailing various jobs, heists, and schemes that had come to the attention of the head of the family back east. That's where Lander had gotten the idea for most of the dozens of money-making unlawful acts the group had perpetrated, including the latest job to which Chester had recently applied the brakes. Chester, who had clearly become Lander's apprentice, whistled slowly when the old man finished his story and finally took a long pull from his own glass of whiskey. This time he felt it go down more smoothly. He had a new respect for his mentor and an appreciation that bordered on love for the woman.

"Those recipes were all really good!" It was Richards, fixated on Mrs. Lander's cooking, and breaking the repose in a way only Don Richards could.

"Do you ever think of anything other than food?" Chester asked, playful.

"Sure," his friend said, "I think I'll have another drink," and he polished off what was left of his bourbon and hoped for a refill. Lander obliged, with a little less of the liquid this time, and brought the conversation back around to the beginning. The new information, gleaned in the last couple of hours, shined a whole new light on the process.

"The folks back east said the Aztec and Mayan artifacts in that Mexican museum are worth millions," he said as Richards spit a spray of just-drank bourbon into his lap, "and they said security would be nonexistent. This would be an easy in-and-out." He shook his head about both Richards and the mystery of the existence of what was supposed to be nonexistent security measures.

"It will be," Chester interjected, and winked at Richards as he remembered the diner discussion, "on Christmas Eve."

THESE DAYS

"Did your dad ever come to Bring Your Dad to School Day? They sat in a booth, by a window, at the Nut Tree Restaurant.

"You mean Career Day?" she corrected him.

"Sure" was his reply.

The dog, as content as she could be, had stretched her legs, sniffed around, then peed. Now she lay flat on her back, hind legs spread, fast asleep, and bathed in the sun's rays that poured through the rear window of the Wagoneer.

The waitress had just dropped off water and the mini loaves of bread for which the restaurant was famous. Leland and Denny were holding hands again. *When did that happen?* he thought. Did he reach for her hands? Did she reach for his? He couldn't remember how it came about and he didn't care. He just knew he liked that it had.

"My dad came to my school a couple of times," Denny said, answering the original question. "The first time was when I was in the third grade; he was a cop, actually a detective."

"Your dad was a cop?" he asked, not knowing why or if he cared and also not remembering if she had already imparted this information.

"Until I was ten," she answered, not sure if she had already mentioned this fact about her family. "The kids, actually one kid, didn't believe him at first because he came to school in a suit. Timmy

Solomon, the class buffoon," she added disdainfully under her breath, still put off by the thought of someone she went to school with decades before. "He told me my dad couldn't be a cop because he didn't wear a uniform and that his dad was the fire chief and he always wore his uniform." She said it like an obnoxious, know-it-all, ten-year-old jackanapes would say it.

Leland, caught off guard, laughed, but his mouth was closed, so it came out as a snort.

"Did you just snort?" Denny asked, her mouth forming a big, sweet smile.

"I believe I did," he said, buttering a piece of bread, "but you have to admit that was a snortable comment."

She nodded, admitting it. "I thought so too"—she looked at him—"now *and* then." She turned her head and looked out the window, the memory coming more sharply into focus. "And, by the way, so did my dad, who happened to overhear the little creep."

"What did he do?"

"He walked right up to Timmy, pulled his suit coat to the side, and showed the brat his shield and holstered gun. Then he told that little Solomon creep to go sit down and keep his little pie hole shut."

Leland snorted again. "He said *pie hole*?"

"I'll never forget it," she said, grabbing a slice of bread for herself.

"Your dad was a cop." This time Leland said it as a statement.

THOSE DAYS

"We took a left here last time," Don Richards said from the passenger seat. Without having to think about it, Chester knew his friend was right. He also knew Don didn't have the assistance of a map, didn't need one. Don Richards wasn't a lot of things, but he also was a lot of things. Loyal was one, and Leland thought that was a critical attribute. He also marveled at Don's ability to know where he was, where he was going, and exactly the best way to get from one place to the other. It was as if the bigger boy, now young man, had maps in his head and a photographic memory to accompany them. He had never been physically lost in his life, and Chester supposed he never would be.

"You're right," he said, and turned left.

Staring straight ahead, Richards smiled. He knew he wasn't the smartest guy around—*that* honor went to the person driving the car, but he also was confident that he brought quite a bit to the table. He was strong—"strong like bull," his mother would always say. He had extraordinary stamina, and for some reason he always knew where he was going and exactly the best way to get there. He also was well aware of the fact that acting dumber than he really was at various times could bring levity to certain situations, comic relief. He was content to give some people the wrong impression, especially if it meant he could stay in the room when important matters were being discussed. He didn't really care if everybody trusted him, but it mattered deeply that Chester did.

"About another mile and a half, and then we make a right."

"Got it. Thanks." Chester drove on.

They made great time and, as expected, the streets were deserted when they made the first pass by the museum. The street lamps were still lit, but Chester thought they shone a bit less brightly. Maybe it was because there were fewer cars on the street and, more precisely, no cops to potentially see them. Whether it was luck, timing, great planning, or a combination of the three, he felt confident the job would go off without a hitch. And it did for the first seventeen minutes. Chester and Don had gathered up most of the relics and secured them safely inside two large black duffel bags. *Excellent but not perfect timing,* thought Chester as he checked his watch and readied himself to collect the coup de grace, the obsidian monkey. He chuckled softly thinking of Don calling the artifact obscene, partly because it was funny and partly because as Chester looked at it up close, it wasn't an unsuitable description.

He knew the monkey was much heavier than any other piece in the museum, but he wasn't sure by how much. Dropping it would be disastrous, and they couldn't be 100 percent sure it wasn't attached to some kind of alarm. Chester took a couple of deep, cleansing, mind-clearing breaths and mustered up all his concentration. Then he slowly reached for the statue.

"Pssst." It was Richards, more loudly than need be. At the unexpected sound, Chester figuratively almost jumped out of his skin and literally nearly knocked the monkey over. He turned and glared at his accomplice but didn't say a word, didn't have to. Twenty feet away Don Richards comically stood like an Aztec warrior, a basket on his head, a length of bamboo in his right hand, thrust forward like a spear. He, of course, had a big smile on his face. Chester slowly mouthed the word *asshole,* and the smile quickly disappeared. Chester took an extra second to compose himself, inhaled another calming breath, and turned back to the task at hand. Richards quickly put the props back where he had found them.

Finally, everything found its proper place in the bags that now rested in the car's trunk, and the thieves, after a punch to the shoulder and a sheepish apology, were back on the road. No issues at the border, in fact the guard (not Emmett Lander) didn't even try to stifle a yawn as he gave a cursory glance at their IDs and waved them into the night.

"Lander said this stuff was worth millions." Richards broke the silence that had enveloped them for about fifty miles.

"Antiques," Chester corrected him, "and yes that is indeed what he said."

"How much do you think we'll get?" Richards asked the question he'd been thinking about since the job began.

"Enough" was all Chester said. An answer to a question that hadn't even crossed his mind.

THESE DAYS

The rain pelted the roof, louder now than it seemed to be when Leland first plopped down amid the boxes and boxes of magazines. He couldn't seem to put a finger on exactly when he had arrived at his father's old house and just how long he'd been sitting among all the memories in the attic. He couldn't recall driving over and couldn't recollect why he decided to come in the first place. He thought he remembered dropping Denny and Potter off at his house, but he couldn't be entirely sure. Like a number of recent occurrences, it all seemed sudden, disjointed, surprising. It was strange on one hand and all too familiar on the other.

The attic smelled like must and cedar, dust and paper, and now rain. Leland closed his eyes and tried to picture his old man, Chester David, up here, conceivably stuffing cartons, perhaps arranging periodicals, maybe even hiding from his mother. Was his dad up here reveling in the deception perpetrated on all those lazy, trusting souls who bought his travel guides, or did he sit up here enveloped in the guilt Leland thought any right-thinking person, so deeply involved in a massive scam, must feel. Eyes still closed he shook his head, saddened by the fact and saddled with the knowledge that he didn't know his father well enough to have a clue as to the answers.

He lay flat on his back and opened his eyes, looking up at the inside of the house's roof. The knots in the two-by-fours looked back.

So did a dozen or so photographs, pictures Leland had never laid eyes on before. He hadn't seen them because he had spent so little time up in the old attic of this old house. As a kid he was never allowed up here, and when he summoned up his preteen courage and tried to sneak in, he found the door locked tight, the fortress impenetrable. He had asked his mom and dad what was in the attic and why it was off-limits and got a lot of "nothing" and "because." At first, the curiosity nagged at him like the itch of a mosquito bite, but he eventually stopped wondering and finally quit caring. When his parents passed and the mystery that was the attic was unveiled, he spent all his time looking down at what was on the floor, not up at what was taped to the ceiling.

Leland tried to focus on the photos and, in doing so, imagined his dad in the exact same prone position. Was Chester trying to remember something or hoping to forget? Leland got to his feet and found an empty wooden crate, not for once wondering why there happened to be one empty box in a room full of containers crammed with *Look*s, *LIFE*s, *Travel & Leisure*s, *National Geographic*s, and *Town and Country*s. He turned the box over, stood on its solid bottom, and got a closer look at the pictures. He saw his mom and dad smiling broadly in one. *Were they ever really that happy together?* he thought as his eyes lingered. In the next photo, his mom and dad were joined by his father's best friend, Uncle Don, and a happy buxom brunette he didn't recognize.

"You look so young and happy," he said out loud, "carefree." They were kneeling among dozens of what looked like Mexican artifacts. Leland wracked his brain trying to remember a story, told by his mother, father, or Uncle Don, about a south-of-the-border adventure or vacation, but nothing came to mind. He tried to remember seeing any of the inanimate objects pictured in the photograph displayed around the house and again came up blank. The group had wrapped left arms around waists, Don Richards on one end, the girls in the middle, and his dad on the other end. Because Chester was on the far end of the frame, neither of his arms interlocked with the others, but his hands weren't free. He held an object. Leland squinted and decided it was an almost life-sized black monkey. His eyes could have been playing tricks on him, but Leland swore it looked like his dad was about to hand the stone statue over to whoever stood behind the camera.

THOSE DAYS

Time passed rather quickly in the weeks—in fact, months, since the Mexico job, and Chester hadn't heard a word from Emmett Lander. Not a peep from the old man, but he wasn't worried. Lander had told them to lay low, stay out of trouble, and do the things "you young people do." That was exactly how he had put it. "I'll be in touch" was the last thing the old man had said after they made the drop. Chester remembered holding the obsidian monkey, still feeling how heavy it felt in his hands. Thinking back, he wondered if it was the weight of the carved stone, the burden of knowing he had graduated into a criminal realm so far beyond swiping baseball cards, picking pockets, and cracking home safes, or a combination of both. He knew for sure he was good at it and careful. He wasn't impulsive, felt no desire to be impressed with himself, and understood how important that was to a successful crime. He also knew keeping his circle of confidants small was important—critical, actually—and that's why it bothered him when Don Richards introduced the girls into their lives.

"The old man said to 'do what young people do,'" Richards had said as a way of convincing Chester to go on the double date, "and young people of one sex spend time with young people of the opposite sex."

"Thank you, Dear Abby." Chester had chided his matchmaking friend before keeping his misgivings to himself and giving in to the double date. Then he went on a second, a third, and finally a fourth before asking Lucille Heller if she'd like to have dinner and a movie without the company of Don Richards and Rachel "Rickie" Chisum. So over time the gang of two doubled in size. On occasion Richards, with a hint of worry in his voice, would ask if Chester had heard from Lander, and every time Chester, without concern, said he hadn't. Their mentor had said he would be in touch, and Chester was confident that, when the time was right, he would be. They were all together as a group again when the time was suddenly right.

"He says to meet him at the house tomorrow night and to go ahead and bring the girls."

"Finally," Richards blurted out, sounding a little too relieved. He grabbed his beer, took a long drink, set the bottle down, and looked at Chester. "How did he know about the girls?"

"He knows about everything," Chester answered, without having to think about it.

"Who's *he*?" the girlfriends said in unison.

THESE DAYS

"Watch your head." Leland let go of Denny's hand and pushed open the door that led to the attic. Potter took that as her cue and ran up the six wooden steps.

"After you, girl." Denny giggled and followed the dog.

"After you, girls." Leland brought up the rear and hit the light switch before going up.

"Oh. My. Goodness," Denny said as she looked around the room. Leland had attempted to describe what they were about to encounter on the drive over, but after seeing and hearing her reaction, he realized he had done an inadequate job.

"Remarkable, isn't it?"

"Arrestive" was her one-word reply.

The dog sniffed around a bit, then plopped down, left leg slightly folded so that her paw came to rest under her chest, and stared at the two humans. After deciding not much excitement was imminent, she rose up into a seated position and decided that was the perfect time to bend over and lick her crotch.

"Because she can." Leland put a personal, Potterized finish to the punch line of the old joke about a dog and its private parts. Denny didn't hear or didn't care to comment and continued to survey the premises.

"How many magazines are there?"

"Never actually counted them, but each box holds around fifty, and there are eight hundred and forty-two of those."

"That's like forty thousand," she said, doing the math in her head.

"Give or take twenty-one hundred or so," he said, having already done it, more than once, in his.

THOSE DAYS

"There must be ten thousand dollars here!" Richards exclaimed as he stared at the stacks of money Lander had set in front of him. They had finished dinner, another delicious meal prepared and served by Mrs. Lander, and the girls were now getting better acquainted during the cleanup process in the kitchen.

"Five times that," Chester knew and said. Richards's eyes widened further. He looked at his friend and then at Lander, who nodded in the affirmative.

"*Fifty thousand dollars?*" Richards whispered, amazed, and reached out to touch the money—his money.

"You earned it," Emmett Lander said like a proud papa. "Now let me give you some professional advice. These words of wisdom also come directly from the East Coast." Richards looked up from his money, all ears. "Don't go running around spending it like a lunatic. That's a shitload of money, and if you just go spending it willy-nilly on stuff you don't really need, people are going to take notice, and by people I mean people in *uniforms*. As long as nobody notices, there will be a lot more where that came from."

"More?" Richards looked back down at the bills and then up again at Lander.

"*A lot* more," Lander replied, "just as long as you promise not to be stupid."

"I promise." Two words this time.

Lander put the money in a plain black gym bag and set it on the floor. Richards hugged it with his feet.

"Let's head into the study," Lander offered. "I want to show you something." Chester got to his feet, but Richards remained seated, staring at the bag filled with bills. "That dough isn't going anywhere, son," Lander chided, and Richards rose.

In the study Lander showed the boys a number of newspaper articles describing the heist in Mexico that was now months in the past. "MUSEUM ROBBED!" read one headline, "AUTHORITIES SUSPECT INSIDE JOB IN MEXICO HEIST!" silently screamed another in bold, black letters. "NO NEW SUSPECTS, NO NEW CLUES, STILL NO TREASURE!" stated a third. Lander poured through the articles and pointed out some of the highlights. The crooks had crept in during the dead of night, on Christmas Eve, and emptied the museum of the valuable relics that once were on display. There was no sign of forced entry, no fingerprints, no clues whatsoever on who might have so expertly pulled the caper off. According to multiple reports, the frustration led both local and national authorities to suspect museum employees, security guards, and even local police officers of the deed because of the lack of any evidence pointing to a break in. One official went so far as to speculate that somebody must have either left the door unlocked or that the thief was in possession of a key because—and here Lander read out loud—"there was no other way anybody could have gotten into that building."

"Of course there was," Chester said proudly, remembering how easy it was to pick the lock on the museum door without leaving so much as a scratch. They all had a good laugh.

"The bosses back east are thrilled," Lander said, once the laughter died down. "There will be no shortage of jobs from now on," he added, unnecessarily.

"Mr. Lander?" It was Richards.

"Call me Emmett, son." Lander had grown fond of the boy, who was becoming a grown man right before his eyes. "What's on your mind?"

"Mr. Emmett," Richards stammered, honoring the request but making sure to include the honorific, "would buying a cabin in the mountains be spending my money willy-nilly?"

Lander pondered the question for what felt like a minute. "Why no, my boy," he finally said. "I believe, done right, that would be a perfectly acceptable way to spend your hard-earned money. In fact, I think that's a fine idea."

"I've always wanted a cabin in the mountains," Don Richards said wistfully.

THESE DAYS

"**Y**our dad was the CDD of 'Stars of David' fame?" she asked, making air quotes.

Leland nodded in the affirmative. "Why? Does that mean something to you?"

"Hell, yes! Of course," she answered. "He helped us get through a trip to Canada one time and a visit to the south of France another." She smiled at the memory.

"And exactly how did he do that?" Leland asked, even though he already knew the answer.

"His books, silly. His guides, his travel, restaurant, and hotel tips," she answered so matter-of-factly that Leland actually felt himself blushing, suddenly embarrassed by her "isn't it obvious" tone of voice. "Why are there so many magazines, and why are most horizontal and others vertical?" she asked, as if she was seeing the publications, not again, but for the first time.

"Don't know." He offered an honest shrug. "That's one of the things I wanted you to see."

"Fascinating," she said.

Was it? he thought.

Denny started another trip around the boxes in the room. Sensing a change in the mood, Potter rose to her feet, wagged her tail, and found the woman's side. "What do you think, girl?" Denny said absentmindedly as she reached down to scratch the Berner behind her left ear. "Maybe he was just a hoarder, one of those people who can't throw anything away." She tested the theory by saying it out loud to the dog, to Leland, and to herself.

"You mean like those crazy people who bury themselves alive in their homes because they can't find a way out through all the junk?" The dog looked at Leland and then back at Denny, who was looking at one of the neatly packed boxes.

"Exactly," she said, but her tone combined with her expression belied the fact that she barely believed it. "One of *those* people." She continued anyway.

"Specific only to certain publications and nothing else." He poked a few more holes in her theory. "A selective hoarder."

She looked at Leland and shrugged.

"There was barely anything left in the house when Mom left, and Dad kept it that way until the day he died." Leland took another look around the attic himself. "Except up here."

"What's this?" she asked, changing the subject and pointing to an unopened leather case behind a couple of boxes in the corner of the attic.

"No idea," he answered, walking over.

THOSE DAYS

C hester David had always loved American crime stories. As a kid because they fascinated him, and as he got older, he paid attention to keep an eye on the competition. Some of those tales proved more interesting than others, like when he became aware of the first confirmed aircraft-hijacking attempt, which took place during a Peruvian revolution in 1931. An American pilot, flying a Ford Tri-Motor, was approached by armed revolutionaries while on the ground. He refused to fly the men anywhere, and after a multiday standoff, the would-be skyjackers happily announced that the revolution had ended successfully and they would gladly let the pilot and his aircraft go if he would agree to fly one of their group to Lima. To that demand he quickly acquiesced. Forty years later the United States was in the early stages of what would become the "golden age of skyjacking."

It all gave Chester an idea, and by the time he mentioned it to his friend Don, he had a plan. It would involve just the two of them—Lander wouldn't know—and after Richards considered that for a moment, he informed his pal that he was all ears. If it was a plan devised, researched, and pulled together by Chester, then Richards had full confidence it would work. Chester laid out the details and put together a timetable. His buddy had already become somewhat of a legend in the mountain community he sometimes called home.

The operation's success relied on Richards's geographical gift. It was a skill, an art, a cartographical competence that Chester didn't have. For the job he had in mind, he knew he needed that skill more than ever. He poured Richards a shot of tequila, slid it in front of him, and told his friend what was expected of them both. In the next ten months or so, Chester would learn to skydive, and Richards would become intimately acquainted with the terrain between Seattle, Washington, and Reno, Nevada. They toasted, clinked glasses, and drank.

THESE DAYS

The dog wandered over and gave the object a quick sniff. Finding nothing particularly captivating, she walked away disinterested. Denny and Leland disagreed with her assessment and squatted in front of a brown leather attaché. Chester guessed it was close to eighteen inches wide, stood about a foot high (not counting the handle), and was probably three to four inches deep. Upon closer inspection he noticed detailed, most likely done by hand, American Indian or Aztec designs etched into the top and bottom of the case. On either side of the handle was a latch that would open when the correct three numbers were dialed up on the combination locks adjacent to them. He picked up the briefcase and gently shook it. It was light, but it wasn't empty.

"What do you think the combination is?" Denny asked without taking her eyes off the object.

"No telling," Leland replied.

"What do you think is in there?"

"No telling."

"Try one, two, three on one side and four, five, six on the other," she said, her first inquiry. He did without success, but the suggestion of the sequence gave him an idea. He spun the numbers he thought might be correct into place, but again the locks didn't budge.

"What was that?" she asked, finally looking at Leland again.

"My dad's birthday month, day, and year." He shrugged his shoulders, disappointed because he was certain those would work.

"Maybe it's your mom's birthday," she said, with a bit of hope in her voice.

"Not likely," he said, instantly dashing whatever hope she may have had, but it didn't discourage her.

"Try yours," she said, as if she had found the goose that laid the golden egg. He did, wondering if those six digits would open the case.

"This is silly. It's not like we're sneaking around trying to break into someone else's property." He said, even though he felt they kind of were. "Let's just call a locksmith." He started to remove the case from his lap. Denny reached out and touched the top of his right hand.

"Just *try* your birthday," she implored.

He spun the digits into place, knowing it was an effort only done to appease her. He had already changed his mind and decided there was no way the combination would be that simple.

Click. One latch released. *Holy crap,* Leland thought, surprised and elated, *that was it!*

"Holy shit!" Denny exclaimed when the second latch popped open. "That was it!"

Leland lifted open the leather box. The top section featured two foldout pockets, the kind that would hold letter- or legal-sized documents or folders. On the outside of the face was a place for a pen or two, another the perfect size to hold business cards, and a third that was a clear plastic slot meant to display identification. All three were as empty as the folders.

"Once upon a time, I invented a device that would keep people from stealing a case like this," Leland started to say.

"What?" Denny interrupted, still examining the case.

"Never mind," Leland stopped the story of the failed briefcase alarm system midthought. Unlike the top compartment, the bottom part of the case was a simple storage space, no pockets, no places to hold anything in place. Equally unlike the top of the case, this section was occupied.

"Cool" was what Denny said as she started to reach in.

"Careful," he cautioned. She was.

THOSE DAYS

T he sign read simply, "Alister McAlister's Flights of Fancy" with a picture of a smiling skydiver and an arrow pointing the way. Chester took the right turn and, after a mile or two, drove right up to a Williams Scotsman portable office trailer. There were two doors with accompanying metal steps, and between the doors was another sign, remarkably similar to the one on the side of the highway, telling all who cared that this was the place. Chester got out of the car and looked around. There was one other car, a rusting Oldsmobile 88, parked in front of the trailer. Chester assumed—correctly, as it turned out—that the bucket of bolts belonged to Alister McAlister himself. As he turned from right to left and faced away from the office, he noticed a dirt airstrip and an airplane. Chester had done some research, and to him the plane looked to be a Cessna 182 Skylane, a fairly standard aircraft used for skydiving. The plane wasn't as beat up as the automobile, but from where Chester stood, it looked like it needed a paint job at the very least.

"She ain't all that pretty, but she gets the job done." Chester hadn't heard either of the office doors open, but open they had, and out had come Mr. McAlister. "Can I help you, son?" he asked, even though he appeared to be not much older than Chester.

"I'd like to learn to skydive," Chester answered.

"Then you've come to the right place." A wad of tobacco juice left his mouth and hit the ground, providing the punctuation mark.

"Good to know," Chester said, and then hocked a nice-sized loogie of his own. Neither man smiled.

Over the course of the next few weeks, Chester paid several more visits to the slightly unsettling Alister McAlister. He learned the basic ins and outs of propelling oneself from a perfectly good airplane. He also learned that Alister McAlister was actually Alan Mackson, a former member of the army's 101st Airborne Division, trained at Fort Campbell, Kentucky. He claimed to have been honorably discharged from that post, and while there may have been some doubt in Chester's mind about that, there was no doubt at all that the guy was an asshole.

Free-fall jumping was the goal, but Alister, or Alan, informed Chester that the first time he exited the aforementioned Cessna, it would be by virtue of a tandem jump. Mackson claimed he got a better feel for the student that way, which, on its surface, made Chester more than a little uncomfortable, but he agreed anyway. So up they went.

The two men were strapped together as the plane rose to a height in excess of twelve thousand feet. Chester was nervous, but only a little, and was thinking about how pretty and peaceful everything looked as he stared out the space that at one time held a door.

One second he was in the plane, and the next second he wasn't.

In the sessions leading up to the first jump, the teacher promised he had told the student everything to expect when propelling oneself into the wild blue yonder. But no words could have adequately prepared Chester for those initial sensations. The wind hit him in the face and pushed his slightly too big goggles up the bridge of his nose. He knew it was cold but honestly couldn't tell for sure if they were rising or falling, if he was holding his breath or screaming. Those thoughts had barely crossed his mind when Mackson pulled the rip cord. Later Chester would swear he immediately, and almost simultaneously, felt three things. The first was an excruciating pain in his right testicle. He was also almost certain he felt the guy on his back, his instructor, laughing, and the third thing Chester felt was the uncontrollable urge to puke from the pain, which he did. That morning's breakfast flew upward out of his mouth, and both Chester and Mackson had the presence of mind to turn their heads away from the vomit. Chester sensed Mackson's body alternately heaving away and then into his own body and knew for sure the dickhead was laughing. Minutes—or was it seconds or hours?—later they were on the ground again.

"Woo hoo!" screamed the instructor after unhooking the apparatus that contained the chute. "That was even better than I had hoped." He slapped his knee and then slapped his student on the back. Chester, having regained the feeling in his right nut and his composure, maintained the anger he felt throughout the fall. He took two steps away from Alan Mackson and then, mustering all his martial-arts training, spun, extending his right leg, and kicked the prick in the balls. Mackson doubled over in pain and shock, and when he did, Chester delivered a blow to the face that both broke the instructor's nose and knocked him out cold. A week later, Chester delivered the ultimate kick in the nuts, giving Alister McAlister's Flights of Fancy exactly *zero* stars in an updated version of the "Spills, Chills, and Thrills" edition of his travel guides. Then he found a new skydiving instructor who mentioned, on their first meeting, that extra padding around the groin area is always a good idea.

THESE DAYS

Leland stared at the contents inside the open case. He didn't blink as his eyes went from one item to the next and back again. He couldn't speak; he could barely breathe. Denny whistled one long, lingering note.

"For fuck's sake." Leland had finally found his breath and his voice.

"This is unbelievable!" Denny added, post whistle. Leland hated that particular superlative, felt it was almost always overused, but he found himself agreeing that this was one of those rare times that the five-syllable word was apropos. They were looking at what appeared to be a march through the history of his father's life, one special piece of memorabilia at a time. The first thing that captured both Leland's and Denny's attention was a brightly colored LP jacket, mostly yellow, featuring the four familiar faces of Dorothy, the Cowardly Lion, the Scarecrow, and, with hatchet in hand, the Tin Man. Above the pigtail-coiffed girl's head were the words in yellow, blue, green, and red: *The Wizard of Oz*. Denny reached into the case with her right hand and pulled the keepsake out for a closer look.

"I think it's an original," she said, looking up from Frances Gumm, aka Judy Garland's face, to Leland's. In the upper right-hand corner, Leland noticed the MGM logo above the words, "Long Playing

33⅓ rpm Recorded." Denny added, "The actual record is inside." Her voice bristled with anticipation.

The recording was still in its original packaging, apparently never subject to the prick and sting of a record player's needle. The song list on the label indicated this particular recording featured a combination of music and dramatic selections from the 1939 motion picture. The year 1956 was stamped on the A-side label.

"Put it back," Leland said softly. Denny obliged and grabbed a small, browning manila envelope in its stead.

"I wonder what this is?" she asked as she pinched what was inside the envelope with her thumb and forefinger and gently pulled it clear. Leland recognized it immediately and didn't know whether to laugh or cry, so he did neither. B. D. Beck Elementary School—read the bold, black letters at the top of the thick, once-white and now yellowing transcript. "Grade: 1st. Teacher: Mr. Conley" was also printed above a list of subjects with a letter grade assigned to each. They both noticed a slightly faded handwritten capital *A* in each box except the two marked Citizenship and Attendance. Each of those earned an *S*.

"Kudos, genius," Denny said sarcastically.

"My first straight-*A* report card," Leland said, the words with a mix of embarrassment and pride, "and maybe my last," he added with a smile. "Why would you hang on to that?" he asked his father's memory, already guessing the answer.

"What else do we have in here?" Denny asked, refusing to engage in Leland's reverie. What else they had was a two-inch cotton-and-polyester black belt—the kind owned and worn by people who had mastered various martial-arts disciplines, and three, obviously old, certainly original, more than likely very valuable, baseball cards. One was a 1909–1911 Christy Mathewson T206 Piedmont Portrait, another was a Cy Young 1911 D304 General Baking Company Bruners Butter Crust SGC 84 7, and the third was a seemingly brand-new, mint-condition 1952 Topps Mickey Mantle Rookie Card that pictured the New York Yankee great holding a yellow bat and resting it on his right shoulder. His eyes appeared to gaze up and off to the right, perhaps looking at a pretty girl in the stands, or maybe seeing the hall of fame career ahead that would make him one of baseball's most famous players.

"Those are worth a lot of money." Denny stated the obvious.

"Six figures as a starting point," Leland agreed.

"For the Mantle card alone," Denny added; Leland was well aware the girl knew her stuff.

The last keepsake was the hardest to identify and explain. It was a clean, crisp twenty-dollar bill, serial number C 13871653 A, encased in clear Plexiglas.

THOSE DAYS

C hester looked at his watch; the second hand ticked left to right until it joined the minute hand and pushed it to 8:00 p.m. straight up. He shoved open the rear door of the Boeing 727-100 aircraft. The night air was cold—he knew it would be—and the wind and rain smacked him in the face. He was alone, looking out and then down toward the ground that he knew was some ten thousand feet below. The pilot, copilot, flight engineer, and one stewardess were, as instructed by him, in the cockpit with the door closed.

Chester had allowed everyone else, including the other thirty-six passengers aboard Northwest Orient Airlines flight 305, off the plane after they landed and taxied to a remote spot at the Seattle-Tacoma Airport. The jet had been refueled, Chester's demands met ($200,000 dollars in "negotiable American currency" and four parachutes), and the five people left on board took off for Mexico just before 7:40 p.m.

While waiting for his ransom, Chester outlined his southerly flight plan to the pilot and crew with explicit instructions to fly the plane no higher than ten thousand feet, at the minimum speed possible to avoid stalling. Chester also demanded the wing flaps be lowered to fifteen degrees, the cabin remain unpressurized, the landing gear locked in the takeoff/landing position, and the rear exit door open with its stairs extended.

"All doable," the pilot, nameplate reading "Scott" pinned to his shirt, had responded knowing the "nut case" making demands, who claimed to have a bomb within his attaché case. He hadn't seen it, but the stewardess had, describing it as "brown." The pilot decided the threat was credible. He told the hijacker, under the specific configuration Chester requested, the plane would only be able to fly about a thousand miles, so they would have to land at least once to refuel again. After several minutes they all agreed the place to do that should be the airport in Reno, Nevada. Chester did his best to conceal a wry smile when the city he knew so well was mentioned. In reality he couldn't care less where these people thought the plane should refuel. He'd be long gone by then.

"Doable," the captain repeated, "except for the aft door remaining open with the stairs extended. HQ says it's too risky to fly this thing that way."

Knowing the pilot and the bozos at "HQ" were full of crap, Chester shrugged his shoulders.

"OK," he said simply, then added, "I know for a fact that's not the case, but fine." He was well aware that he could open the door and deploy the stairs himself once they were up in the air. Like most everything in Chester David's life, he knew what he was doing because he had read, studied, practiced, and then committed to memory everything he needed to know about making a briefcase look like a bomb, writing a ransom note, and first hijacking and then jumping from a passenger plane.

"Everything all right back there?" Scott's voice called over the intercom. Chester stared at it and said nothing. "We've been alerted up here to an air-pressure change in the cabin. Do you require assistance?"

Never trust a man with two first names, the criminal with two first names had quickly thought upon seeing the nameplate for the first time. "Just fly the plane," he barked back curtly.

During the entire process, Chester was dressed neatly in a dark suit, white dress shirt, a skinny black necktie fastened by a mother-of-pearl pin, loafers, and a lightweight black raincoat. He added a pair of dark sunglasses to conceal his eyes and make it harder for the folks he came across to identify him later. Once alone, and after taking off from the Sea-Tac Airport, he shed the clip-on tie and the mother-of-pearl tie clip, both of which had been worn hundreds of times by his dear old dad, and left them on seat 18C. He then unwrapped one of the four parachutes, cut the shroud lines from its canopy, and left it, along with another, unopened chute.

He had then secured the remaining two parachutes to his back and strapped the ten thousand twenty-dollar bills to his chest. He made his way back to the open door and the wind and the rain. Chester David looked at his watch one more time. One second it read 8:13; the next second he jumped.

THESE DAYS

"What were the holidays like at your house?" They sat on the attic floor, Denny Indian-style and Leland with legs outstretched.

"What do you mean?"

"I mean everything." She looked at him. "Christmas mornings, Easter egg hunts, Thanksgiving dinners." She paused. "You know, holidays."

He didn't answer right away, maybe feeling a little guilty because Christmas mornings were the first thing that crossed his mind. It reminded him he was a lucky kid, almost everything he had asked for waited under the tree.

"I never got a pony," he said curtly, without looking at her, "if that's what you're getting at."

"Whoa, cowboy, *pun* absolutely intended." She punched him on the thigh. "Why so defensive?"

"Sorry," he said honestly.

"Did you ever *ask* for a pony?" she chided him.

"No," he said honestly, bracing for another shot to the thigh that never materialized. A few seconds of comfortable silence passed between them.

"I always thought everything was completely normal." Leland spoke first when the conversation resumed. "I had birthday parties,

Easter egg hunts, inside when it was too cold, outside when it wasn't, and plenty of presents on Christmas morning." Denny watched him and nodded. Leland kept going. "It was usually just me, my mom, and my dad. I remember my dad's best friend, my 'Uncle Don,' being there sometimes too. A bunch of friends always came to my birthday parties, and I always had plenty of buddies to call and tell them what I got for Christmas."

"Me too." Denny was looking off in the distance, remembering her own good times. "My dad always did his best to make special occasions really special, especially after my mom left."

"How old were you?"

"Little," she answered quickly, sending Leland the message that that was all the answer he was going to get on that particular subject. "Thanksgiving was the best." She smiled at a happier memory. "My old man loved to cook a bird."

"We always went out." Leland didn't smile. He was the envious one now.

"On *Thanksgiving?*" Denny was incredulous.

"My mom wasn't much of a cook, and my dad didn't." He shook his head. "Besides, he said it gave him a chance to rate a new restaurant every year."

"Makes sense," Denny said, but "That's a little sad" is what she meant.

"Except one."

"Except one what?"

"Except one Thanksgiving." Leland remembered. "1971. It was just me and mom." He tried to recall if there were others, but at the moment that was the only year he could come up with.

THOSE DAYS

Chester found himself alone and in the dark again. He chuckled silently to himself thinking about all the bedroom closets, back alleys, and pitch-dark shadows in and under which he had spent so many minutes of his life. He absentmindedly rubbed a coin between his thumb and forefinger. He had done that before as well—once upon a time with a piece of scrimshaw, these days with a quarter. He had done it so often, in fact, that just about the only thing still identifying the silver piece as a quarter was its size. Chester had rubbed away "Liberty" and "In God We Trust," as well as the four-number date at the bottom of the face of the coin. He was currently working on the other face, that of George Washington. At the moment all that was left was the tip of the great man's nose and the curl at the bottom of his wig. Chester imagined after a few more nights like this one, those would be history as well. He thought next about his friend Don Richards. The two young men had been all-in from the beginning and were getting rich because of it, but now there were girls involved too, and that's what Chester was thinking about that night, in his mind, in the dark. He could trust Don, would trust him with his life; he just had, and that wasn't the first time. But could the same be said about Richards's girlfriend, Rickie, and her friend, Lucille, who just happened to be sleeping in his bed in the next room? Could their silence be bought? Could they be convinced that discretion was indeed the perilous path everyone needed to follow? Richards had assured Chester over and over again that there was nothing to worry about, which, of course, made Chester worry all the more.

He recalled a weekend, not all that long ago, that found the four of them enjoying the comfort of Don's mountain chalet. It was a lazy morning after a late night, and Richards had awakened with a self-described "*unsatiable* hunger." He announced to the group the only thing that could satisfy it was a sub from his favorite deli. Grudgingly, Leland and the girls agreed to go along. In the dark he flipped the coin and began to rub the other side. For the moment he found himself back in the tiny restaurant, around a table full of friends.

Richards ordered the Italian sandwich and immediately dug in. Leland remembered Lucille barely sipping a cup of chicken soup, *his* hands around a cold bottle of Coca-Cola, and Rickie nursing a bottle of beer she brought from the house. He also thought about the conversation that followed.

"A little hair of the dog," Rickie said, tilting the neck of the beer bottle toward the others in a toast.

"I can't believe you guys aren't hungry," Richards managed to say through a mouthful of salami, mortadella, capicola, and provolone. A sliver of shredded lettuce hung from the side of his mouth.

"God, Donny!" Rickie scolded.

"You shouldn't talk with your mouth full," chided Lucille.

"Sorry." Richards picked the lettuce and dropped it on the butcher paper. "But you guys are really missing out."

"Let me guess," Chester remembered saying, "the combination of the salty, slightly spicy meats, mingled with the mellow provolone and topped off by the symphony of oregano, oil, and vinegar make for a biting, yet balanced experience. A perfectly harmonious way to handle your hunger."

"What he said." Richards added.

They all laughed.

"Maybe they should call this joint *A Capella*," Rickie added.

"More like *Ahhh Capicola*," Richards said with a belch.

"I have an idea." It was Lucille, and she was looking right at Chester.

Back in the present, Chester let loose a light chuckle and realized that complicating matters was the fact that he found himself fond of Lucille, very fond, and he was pretty sure she felt the same way. He continued to rub the quarter—it soothed him, eased his mind—and then he got up and got the handgun from the safe, hidden under the floorboards in his office. He set the coin on the corner of his desk and replaced it in his hand with the pistol's custom silencer. Softly snoring in the bedroom, Chester followed her sounds there. He had moved silently for so long, it cost him no effort to do it again. He knelt by her sleeping form, put the muzzle of the gun against her forehead, and cocked the trigger. Lucille opened her eyes at the sound and then slowly lifted them to get a glimpse of the gun's barrel pressed to her skin. Much to Chester's surprise, and satisfaction, she smiled.

"What are you doing, baby?" she asked sleepily.

"Hey, gorgeous," he answered softly, keeping the gun to her soft skin with the hammer pulled back. "We're in this shit knee-deep now. You know that, right?"

"Is this you asking if you can trust me?" she asked, with a strong, steady voice.

"That's exactly what this is." His voice was equally firm.

With her left hand, she reached up and put her fingertips on the top of the barrel of the silenced handgun. The slight smile stayed, lifting the corners of her mouth. Chester immediately wanted to kiss her. Instead she helped him lower the gun until it was even with her lips; then she seductively wrapped them around the well-oiled barrel. Chester slowly eased the hammer back into place and allowed himself a slight smile too. She slid the barrel out of her open mouth and reached for his crotch with her right hand.

"Come back to bed," she said, pulling him toward her.

Chester could never quantify how much he liked her in that moment. In fact, he surmised later that he fell madly in love with her right then and there. At the time he didn't know, didn't care, that she would one day become his wife and the mother of his only son. He could never have imagined she would be the impetus behind his mostly fictional restaurant-and-resort review anthology. It was Lucille's idea for him to start the enterprise as a cover for his clandestine, conniving exploits, and it was brilliant. What he also couldn't have known as he was making love to Lucille that night was that he would never like her, ever again, as much as he liked her in that instant. But like her or not, he realized he could, and always would, trust her.

THESE DAYS

B ack in the comfort of his own home, Leland stood at his desk, Denny by his side, the dog currently not visible but surely somewhere nearby. They must have left everything they had discovered back in his old man's attic because, like the dog, the memorabilia were nowhere to be found. His desk was surprisingly and uncharacteristically uncluttered, and on it, conspicuously displayed, was the note written by his Uncle Snoshu. Before bringing up the note and soliciting Denny's opinion about its meaning, he thought he'd lean in for a kiss.

Leland couldn't get over how strange he thought it all had become. He spent his adult life mostly unconcerned about his personal life, or lack thereof. Comfortably insouciant about not having a playmate, date, or significant other. Suddenly, in a matter of days that felt like hours, occasionally minutes, he found himself crippled with fear over the thought of *not* having this one person in his life. He closed his eyes and took advantage of the chance to gather his thoughts before making the effort to articulate his feelings. A jumble of happy emotions he thought he knew, but still hoped, Denny shared. He was convinced he heard the sonance of a phone with an oddly familiar ringtone somewhere in the distance. Strange, he thought, because he was fairly certain his phone was in his pocket, and he honestly couldn't remember ever seeing a phone in Denny's possession. Phone or no phone, she must have agreed to the kiss because he felt her soft, warm lips.

Suddenly something akin to panic disturbed his senses. Everything that was Denny seemed to dissipate, her essence scattered, ill formed. His anxiety heightened, and his eyes burst open, aware now of an image—he was sure it was her—heading toward a door he didn't remember being there. He tried to move, but it was as if his feet were superglued to the floor. He attempted to reach out, but his hands stayed locked to his side, hundred-pound weights on ten-pound arms. He was immediately reminded of recurring dreams he had as a kid on nights before the final round of a big high-school, college, or statewide golf tournament. Tournaments he always had a chance to win. It was his turn to play, but a hedge, a wall, or a crowd of people always materialized, inhibiting his backswing. No matter where he moved or how hard he tried, he could never take the club back. His frustration grew greater as his efforts proved unsuccessful.

"Where are you going?!" he tried to scream. "Come back!" he cried at the top of his lungs. But words didn't, for some reason *couldn't*, escape his lips. Between his brain and his vocal cords, the pleas were transformed into guttural croaks, all indistinguishable and nowhere near loud enough to attract the attention of the apparition moving farther and farther away. He mustered up one last, heroic effort to come unstuck and follow, to extend his arms and prevent her exit. But it was as unsuccessful as the first. Then she was gone.

Every ounce of his being felt the desire—no, the need—to see Denny King one more time. One second she was there, a constant companion, and in less than an instant, she was gone. Leland's breath left his lungs, and he was certain his heart was no longer whole. Then he opened his left eye. Something in his brain told him he knew where he was, sitting at his desk, head down, right side of his face pasted to the wooden slats. Another part of that same brain screamed, "Don't believe it. She's still here somewhere." Sadly, he knew which part was true. His right hand, pinned underneath his right thigh, was numb from compressed nerves. His mouth was parched, his lips crusty, and dried drool dotted both the wood and a small space between his cheek and chin.

The dog, her paws on the desk, head on her paws, face inches from his, stuck out her pink tongue and licked her master's face. His best guess was that she had been there all along. Denny, on the other hand, was gone, clearly having never really existed in the first place. And even though there most certainly *was* an Uncle Snoshu, there had also never been a note. His hand started the tingle back to normalcy as he forced the different parts of his brain to remember everything about the dream girl—every feature, every sound, every smell, every smile. He also recalled every word on the imaginary note. After he scratched the pup's multicolored snout, he removed his face from his desktop and rubbed the sleep from his eyes. Then he wrote them down, exactly as they were written, at the top of a brand-new page in his moleskin notebook.

"don't be too hard on your old man. he was Doing the Best he Could. celebrate all the days of his life."

"Well I'll be dipped in shit," Leland said out loud, remembering how real the dream felt as well as a phrase his dad would say the few times he seemed caught by surprise. Suddenly he felt like he had a mystery to solve...or create.

"Want to go to Grandpa's, girl?" he asked the dog, already well aware of the answer.

THOSE DAYS

"**S**how me where you found him." Lander was hunched over a map of the states that made up the Pacific Northwest. Richards stood over his left shoulder, Chester his right.

"Here." Don's finger settled on a spot in the southwestern part of Washington state. Chester nodded and shifted his weight. It had been weeks since the night he left the confines of the Northwest Orient airplane and leaped into the rain, the darkness, and an uncertain future. He still felt pain in both his left ankle and his right shoulder.

"What river is this?" Lander's perfectly manicured, comically crooked index finger tapped what actually was a conflux of two bodies of water.

"The big one is the Columbia and the skinny, smaller one is the Washougal," Richards answered.

"And that's where you fellas met up?" Lander asked another question, keeping his finger on the piece of paper and swiveling his head slightly to meet Don's eyes. Without looking away, Richards nudged the old man's fingertip ever so slightly to the north and east on the map.

Chester's mind wandered. The scheme wasn't supposed to involve Lander at all, and originally it didn't. Chester and Don both did their homework, executed each part of the plan with precision, and ended up pulling off one of the most spectacular robberies in American criminal history. They walked away, as yet unapprehended, with a hell of a tale they could never tell and $200,000 they could never spend.

"We need the old man's help." Chester remembered the words that came out of his friend's mouth, a little perturbed because he knew Don was right.

"Give me some of the money." Lander's voice interrupted Chester's memory. The old man pulled away from the table and looked at the two younger criminals. *Here it comes*, Chester thought cynically, the geezer wanting his cut for helping them launder the money.

"Why?" Richards blurted out. Chester shook his head.

"Price of doing business," he said, thinking he knew what Lander was thinking. For his part Emmett Lander just stood there, saying nothing, and looking back and forth at the faces of his criminal team. Several seconds, which felt like forever to Chester, passed.

"What?" Chester inquired of the older gentleman, wincing as he shrugged his shoulders. Now it was Lander's turn to shake his head, and he did that slowly.

"I'm gonna pretend this is just a momentary case of the stupids and *not* an indication that you fellas have so little regard for me."

Chester felt his face go flush. He lowered his eyes and then his head, immediately embarrassed that he had made such an egregious miscalculation. Richards stood still and opened his mouth to speak. No words came tumbling out because he realized he didn't know what to say. As happened so often, when it came to both the spoken and unspoken communication between Lander and Chester, Don Richards had no idea what was going on.

"Please forgive me, sir," Chester mumbled.

"A case of the stupids it was," Lander said, a little louder than necessary. "No harm, no foul," he added, and gave Chester's uninjured shoulder a genuine, loving squeeze.

"What just happened?" Richards asked the room.

"Mr. Lander was about to tell us why he needs some of the money."

"Actually I need you to give me *all* the money." Richards started to protest, but stopped immediately when Chester held up a hand.

"I've already got somebody ready, willing, and able to get you other money you can spend instead of this money that you can't." Lander continued, ignoring the near interruption. "But some of what you got is going back to the great state of Washington. We're about to throw the authorities a curveball." He smiled and got the same reaction from the other two. "Now if you boys are all done freelancing, we've got two more jobs, one on the front burner and one on the back. Quite frankly, fellas, this second caper might just be our last."

The mood in the room had seemingly gone off the rails and then just as quickly righted itself. Chester had the presence of mind to think the more complicated the crime, the better. He had been religious about staying fit, practicing his martial arts and maintaining his expertise. He had also stayed diligent about keeping his fingers and his senses fine-tuned by pulling off jobs, in addition to the high-altitude heist, on his own. The excitement over the more difficult job was tempered slightly by the information divulged that their criminal collaboration might be coming to an end. Chester decided he'd worry about that later.

"We'll need the two of you *and* the girls for the first piece of business." Lander paused ever so slightly to see if there was any objection from the boys about continuing to work with the girls. When he heard none, he continued. "The second job involves just the two of you."

Lander outlined the jobs in chronological order, starting with the theft of what was known as "The Tucker Cross." The piece, a twenty-four-carat-gold artifact with embedded emeralds, was recovered from the wreck of the San Pedro, a ship that was sunk sometime near the end of the sixteenth century. Hundreds of years later, a diver named Tucker had found it as part of a sunken treasure, and even though it was considered by several experts to be priceless, Tucker put a price on it and sold it to a Caribbean government. That very same government was about to put this magnificent find on public display, in a public museum, so the Queen of England could get a very public look at it during her upcoming visit. She'd get a look at something all right, but if Emmett Lander got his way, that something would actually be an amazing lookalike, literally cooked up in his wife Evelyn's kitchen.

THESE DAYS

"You ready, girl?" Leland had unlocked the attic door and was just about to pull it open and climb the stairs. Before hopping in the Jeep and heading over to his dad's place, Leland listened to the message left on his phone. The device had indeed rung, perhaps the impetus that dragged him from a life he would have gladly led despite the fact that it existed only in the deepest recesses of his imagination, and back to the reality he faced. A reality that now seemed far less normal. On the other end of the line was his old friend Jeremy Porter, and his message was short and sweet.

"We're at the Tahoe house, and we haven't seen you in a while. Kelly misses you, and I miss the dog. Any chance you can make the trip our way soon?" Leland just shook his head and smiled.

"We were just there last night," he said to the canine. She looked back at him as if she had no idea what he was talking about, because she had no idea what he was talking about. He'd also been at the foot of these attic stairs before, both in his dream and in real life, and uncertainty about what he might find for real this time filled his mind. But this was the first visit to the attic for the living, breathing Bernese mountain dog, and nothing but excitement filled her mind as a wagging tail would attest. As soon as Leland turned the knob and opened the door, she was clattering up the wooden stairs like there was a squirrel, in tux and tails, tap dancing at the top. Her master followed more slowly.

"Easy," he said, both to the dog and himself. From inside the attic, the pup, who rarely barked, barked. Leland stopped in his tracks at the uncommon sound.

"Denny?" he asked halfway up the stairs, sounding more like a hopeful teenager than a heartsick grownup.

At the top of the stairs, he stood and surveyed the room. At first glance it looked like it had on the few previous visits, but the nocturnal events, just hours in the past, made Leland look with more intent. Just like in his dream, the boxes were still there, dozens of them, but unlike the imaginary scene, the magazines inside those boxes were all arranged in the same fashion, spine up, information about each in plain sight. The dog was sniffing in a corner, and Leland's eyes found her. Next to the pup, hanging from an exposed beam in the ceiling, was a well-worn heavy bag, a foot or two above a once-black, now-gray rubber gym mat. A karate-gi was displayed on a hanger nearby along with a black belt, proudly providing a stark contrast to the rest of the all-white martial-arts uniform. Leland had seen the garb but never his father actually in it. He could picture his dad in it now. The dog looked up, licked its lips, and turned to find something else to sniff.

THOSE DAYS

Chester was alone in the attic of the home he occupied with his wife and their constantly growing, continually curious son, Leland. In front of him was a case he had kept. The meager effects left to him by his father. He hated the case but couldn't bring himself to toss it like he had done with everything else his dad had left behind when he made his untimely, self-inflicted, exit from this earth. Nothing on the outside of the attaché identified it as belonging to either Chester or his not-so-dear, departed dad. Nothing on the inside would help anyone identify the piece of baggage either. That's because, at that exact moment, there wasn't anything inside the case. The thing that Chester *hoped to be* there was, for lack of a more eloquent term, at least one rock. A rock about the size of the scrimshaw and then the quarter he once used to soothe his troubled mind. But the new talisman would have been bright, brilliant, as green as ever, maybe even the largest of the seven emeralds that had been embedded in the Tucker Cross. It was one piece of a piece Emmett Lander had long planned to steal. Like every job, the old man had done his research, planned the robbery, convinced them all it would be easy, and in the end, it was. Easier even than Lander had imagined and most definitely easier to steal than Chester, Richards, and the others had thought it would be. The artifact had been part of a sunken treasure, found then sold, and destined to be housed in a national museum on a tiny island nation. Emmett Lander coveted the booty, and Evelyn Lander worked for years making an incredibly authentic clone cross. Thanks to the perfect combination of cut glass, food coloring, time, temperature, and other ingredients, she had gotten the recipe and the replica just right.

The still nickname-less group, led by Chester, pretended to be couples on vacation, headed to the small spot of land in the Atlantic Ocean. The impressive piece sat on display, awaiting a visit from Queen Elizabeth II, in the center of an open room, in the middle of an unimpressive museum. Lander had mapped out the space for them, and Chester had committed the dimensions to memory. When they arrived, they were surprised, yet delighted, to find the fifteen-by-eighteen-foot space displayed the artifact and nothing else. No mirrors, no cameras, no other visitors, and last, but certainly not least, no guards. Without one worry in the world, one drop of perspiration, or one twitch of a single muscle, Chester deftly made the swap. The rest of the group stood sentry, admiring Chester's technique as well as what was no cheap imitation of the magnificent original. Minutes later they left the room, hours later they left the island, and days later they delivered the goods to the husband-and-wife masterminds.

The emeralds were excised from the twenty-four-karat gold cross; Lander would have that melted down. When Chester and Don arrived at the Lander's home, the jewels were displayed on the kitchen table along with what looked to Chester like about $10,000 in cash. Outside the cross, they looked bigger, more impressive. The money looked like money.

"Will you look at those!" Richards pointed at the emeralds and then slapped Chester on the back. He flinched, then offered a humorless smile. He did as instructed, glancing briefly at the jewels, but then his gaze fell upon Emmett Lander. Something didn't look right, didn't feel right. He didn't say a word, but Richards did.

"It was awesome," he spoke directly to the old man, "this guy here made it look so easy."

Chester silently appreciated the compliment, but he wished his friend would keep his own thoughts to himself. But, of course, he didn't.

"He was like a magician when he made the ol' switcheroo." The admiration punctuated by several hand motions in an attempt to illustrate the technique used by Chester during the heist.

"But honestly he didn't need to be that tricky. We were surprised there was nobody there, no guards, no cameras. It was like they never considered anybody would try to swipe the thing. Or they didn't care." Lander just stared at Richards, unmoved, unimpressed.

Please shut up! Chester thought. His mind raced, *this should have been a celebration. Worthy of congratulations all around, maybe even champagne. So why was Lander so stoic? Why did he look so irascible? Was he mad? Was he envious?*

"It was *so* easy!" Richards added again, and Chester noticed Lander bristle. He wanted to say something to warm the chill in the room, to appease his mentor, cut the tension. He needed to divert the attention away from his role in the heist and heap praise on the Landers. He never got the chance.

"Well, I'm glad to hear it was no skin off your butts." Lander's words were not intended as a compliment. He cleared his throat and took two steps closer to the table. The sinister countenance Chester had noticed, way back when at the Mexican border, was present again. This time in the room. "That means I did *my* job, and maybe, because I did it so well, I should reap the rewards. All of them." With that announcement, Lander swept the emeralds off the table and dropped them into a small leather pouch. He left the cash. Then, without another word or glance toward either boy, he left the room. Chester couldn't help thinking this was the way Lander had always intended it to turn out.

"What the heck just happened?" It was Richards, still oblivious to the hostility that continued to linger in the room—the uneasiness Chester had noticed right off the bat. He couldn't get the look on Lander's face out of his mind. The distance, the coldness, the lack of benevolence and compassion. He had seen that look before, not often but once or twice, in his own father's eyes.

"We just got screwed by somebody we should have known would screw us." Chester spat, heading for the door.

"What do you mean *we, Kemosabe?*" Richards parroted a popular joke; then he scooped up the cash and followed Chester out the door.

THESE DAYS

L eland walked to the center of the room and remembered more of his dream. He looked up to the ceiling, wondering if pictures of his father, mother, and "uncle" would be looking back. They weren't—another difference between reality and fantasy. He knew the dream also revealed a treasure chest, in the form of an attaché case, in another corner of the attic, and that's where Leland's attention went next. A closer examination of that space revealed no such ornate, leather briefcase, but there was one more cardboard box, this one covered and sealed with yellowing packing tape. Leland felt his heart beat faster. On the box's lid, in bold, black, felt-tip-marker-made letters was one word:

LELAND

His knees went weak, and he actually pinched himself to make sure this wasn't a different dream. Satisfied after the intentionally prolonged pressure, he took some of the burden from his weakened joints and knelt next to the cardboard container. The dog trotted up to be by his side. The look on her face corroborated the hope that there might be something exciting or tasty in her future. Her human's expression was much more apprehensive. *How can I want and not want to do something so badly at the same time?* he thought, picking up the box to test its weight. He heard and felt some of the items inside shift, but the receptacle was no trouble for him to lift. He was, however, both troubled by and certain of the knowledge that the contents, though light, were not going to be inconsequential. He used his car key to slice the deteriorating tape that kept the lid on the items, set the box top on the floor, and looked inside.

THOSE DAYS

"I've got to go out of town for a while," Chester sat on the edge of the bed having just pulled on one sock and getting ready to pull on the other.

"What's a while?" Lucille sat, legs crossed at the ankles, her back pressed against the bed's headboard and head resting on a throw pillow embroidered with the words "Hello, Gorgeous." Chester had started calling her that right after they first met and still called her that to this day. He had given her the pillow on a long-ago Valentine's Day, or was it a birthday or anniversary? He tried for a second to remember, but only for a second because he realized it didn't matter now.

"No telling." The other sock now on.

"Business or pleasure?"

"Business *is* pleasure, gorgeous." With that he leaned across the queen-size mattress, kissed his wife on the forehead, and headed for the master bathroom. He hoped the show of affection and the use of the familiar pet name felt and sounded sincere. Her response was an actual sincere smile.

"We need some new restaurants to review," she said to his back. "We're due to publish another volume of the Guides." He grabbed his toothbrush and began to apply the paste, stopped, and stuck his head around the doorframe.

"We haven't been to the Bahamas," he said, "or maybe it's time to update the Midwest. You know, Minneapolis, Detroit, Chicago?" He stopped there and jammed the toothbrush in his mouth.

"I'll pick up some more magazines" was her reply.

Chester thought Lander's latest plan was genius, but after the Tucker Cross betrayal, his trust in the old man was diminished. Lander never mentioned that job or the emeralds again, but Chester never forgot. He was certain Lander would say that it was another one of his "life lessons," but Chester thought that was bullshit. The old geezer had taken him under his wing, taught him a great deal and made him a lot of money to be sure, but in the end Chester realized he was no better, actually probably worse, than most people. Just one more person to *not* put your faith in. Sure Chester could still learn from Lander, still work for him, take his money but he would never trust him again. In fact, he stuck around mostly because of Mrs. Lander. He had faith in her.

Initially he had a couple of misgivings about the current gig and wondered if it could really succeed. As was always the case, Lander came back with more than a dozen reasons why it couldn't fail. It was a bank job, a first for Chester and Don, but both supposed it was far from a first for Lander. Like most of their efforts, this one was concocted by the brains and the boys back east. It had been in the works for a while, and some of the necessary groundwork had already been laid. The most important initial aspect was implanting an employee who could be on the payroll of both the Chicago First National Bank and the New York/New Jersey mob. That had been accomplished months before. The next most important piece of the puzzle fell neatly into place when an office in the building, adjoining the bank, was leased for six months to a small family accounting firm run by two brothers. The third member of that family, a sister, paid for the lease, up front, in cash. They negotiated the lease down a bit because one side of the building shared a wall with the bank, but the management firm got some of that money back because the accountants wanted to be on the first floor. As she counted out the cash, the sister remarked that the family liked that their new place of business was next to a bank because "we might get some walk-ins from next door." The young man executing the lease would always remember her saying that, not because it was particularly enlightening, but because the smile on her face that followed was spectacularly luminous.

The brothers actually liked it because, thanks to an architectural anomaly, there was actually a space, slightly more than eighteen inches' worth of a space, between the two buildings. They would access their side of the gap from the office restroom and enter the bank several floors down in the same space as the vault. A shingle was hung outside the door, and the boys got to work. The "brothers," Chester David and Don "Snoshu" Richards, were hardworking accountants (despite the fact that they never had any customers) by day and construction workers by night. They dismantled the restroom wall, piece by piece, tile by tile, and reconstructed a false front that would fool anyone upon first or even second or third glance. Having been privy to the building plans, Chester knew there was a cranny, in theory wide enough for him to occupy, between the office building and the bank, and he spent several nights testing that premise. He recalled the first few times Snoshu opened up the bathroom wall and Chester entered the breach. He wasn't surprised by the darkness, the dampness, or the distinct aroma of old dirt. He was a little perplexed by the sense of fear that skittered down his neck the first time he crawled inside. He couldn't remember being afraid of anything, even as a kid being bullied or testing his boundaries while breaking and entering, but that first time between the aging Chicago buildings, he sensed he wasn't alone. He knew he was the first two-legged creature in decades to occupy that space, but there had to be critters—six, eight, and million-legged creepy crawlies keeping him company. He "felt" something on his neck, knew something was in his hair, sensed a sting or a bite was eminent, and he couldn't get out of there fast enough.

"What's the matter, tough guy?" Chester remembered Richards sitting on the commode, chuckling.

"Nothing" was his response.

"Hey," Richards added, "what if there's a skeleton buried in there? You know, like in the Poe story 'The Cast of Amontillado'?"

"Cask." Chester couldn't help correcting his friend. "And you're *not* helping."

Thanks to a full-body covering, poisons, and finally, familiarity, Chester got more and more comfortable between the buildings and was soon enough gliding up and down from one point of entry to the other. It was critical that he was careful when dislodging the bricks and opening up the wall that allowed him entry to the vault room. Several bank employees had access to the old black behemoth inside, so deceiving one might be easier than fooling another. Richards showed him the best way to dismantle and then lay just enough bricks to complete the task, and after weeks of practice in the bathroom, Chester felt he was ready for the real thing. Snoshu agreed.

He had insisted to Lander and, by extension anyone who would listen, that he had the skills to crack the vault's combination and gain entry inside. Lander knew he could but assured him that it wouldn't be necessary. Thanks to their inside man, Chester would have the combination long before he executed the plan. Briefly disappointed, Chester's spirits brightened when Lander assured him his lock-picking skills would, in fact, be of use when it came to opening the cash box full of money that would be the target inside the vault.

The team's plant had proven himself to be an exemplary employee, earning praise from coworkers and outstanding performance reviews from the bank manager. He had even gone the extra mile, over time befriending his boss and making it a point to interact socially with the man and his wife. Mondays turned out to be their evening of choice for get-togethers.

It just happened to be a Monday when the bank employee counted exactly four million dollars in cash and stored it in the bank's money cart. He then put the cart, with the cash, in the vault. At five minutes to five, he straightened up his desk, grabbed his coat from the back of his chair, and headed out the door. On the way out, he stuck his head inside his boss's office.

"The wife and I are looking forward to tonight," he said happily.

"Same here," the manager replied. "See you at the restaurant." The employee gave his employer a thumbs up.

"Drinks at six thirty, then dinner," he added, removing his head from the room. After a well-rehearsed beat, he was back.

"Oh, and I didn't tell the wife, but I snagged tickets for the show at the Sutherland Lounge later." The manager stopped midsignature on some document or another, lifted his head, and smiled.

"Who's playing?" he asked expectantly.

"Just the one and only Jimmy McPartland," he said, pulling the tickets from his pocket and waving them triumphantly in the air. McPartland was a native son of Chicago and one of the world's best cornetists. He was also one of the originators, along with Lovie Austin, Gene Krupa, and others, of what was known as Chicago Jazz. He was no longer a spring chicken, but he was still great, and a ticket to any one of his performances was a great get.

"McPartland at the Sutherland?" The manager was suitably impressed. "Can't wait." And he didn't for very long. Customarily the first to arrive and the last to leave, the bank manager slipped on his own overcoat at exactly 5:20 p.m., went through, then locked the door behind him, and headed home to change and give his wife the good news. Chester David was already between the walls.

Just like the skydiving, he had practiced the decent and subsequent ascent dozens and dozens of times before. He knew it only took a matter of minutes to slip past the imaginary skeleton, reach the bottom, and open up the bank side, allowing him access to the vault. On his last visit, he loosened the bricks and expertly set them back into place without sealing them. Every person who had entered the vault room since was unaware that there was anything out of the ordinary. This trip, while familiar, was different than any other. This time Chester would be carrying down a bota bag filled with warm water, a plastic bag containing quick-drying Portland cement, and a trowel. He'd climb back up, face close to one wall, back against the other, with an empty bota bag, an empty plastic bag, a trowel, and two black duffel bags equally full of fifty- and one-hundred-dollar bills amounting to exactly one million dollars.

On Tuesday the employee and the bank manager were back in the boss's office reliving the previous evening of drinks, dinner, and amazing jazz that had lasted well past midnight. Things had gone so well that both couples needed Checker cabs to get home. They were still suffering from mild hangovers when a third employee, as white as a proverbial ghost, breathlessly burst into the office and informed the two gentlemen that the bank had exactly one million dollars less in a locked cart, inside a locked vault, than it had approximately fifteen hours prior.

Of course, the police were called, and eventually all the guards and employees, including the manager and the mob's accomplice, were exonerated thanks to iron-clad alibis. The robbery remained a mystery for days, weeks, and months. By the time detectives got around to canvasing the neighborhood for any clues, the "brother" accountants were long gone. No one was surprised; actually, few could remember exactly when they left. Fewer still could recall ever seeing a customer walk through the door.

THESE DAYS

There weren't any photographs taped to the ceiling of the attic, but there was one staring back at him from the inside the box. He picked it up to get a better look at his mom, his dad, Snoshu, two other women (one old, one much younger), and a black stone monkey. He showed the photo to his four-legged friend.

"Bet you dollars to doughnuts that monkey is made of obsidian." The dog tilted her head and her ears perked up at the sound of the word *doughnuts.* He chuckled at the canine's expression and thought more about the picture, even though it was eerily similar to the one he saw in his dream, he concluded it was the first time he had actually seen his parents in a snapshot together. He recalled pictures of himself at various ages and displaying assorted feats of accomplishments scattered around the house on walls, mantles, and appliances, but he couldn't, for the life of him, recollect any pictures of his mom, his dad, or his mom *and* dad together.

There was one other photograph, this one laying on the bottom of the box. Upon closer inspection Leland realized it was a mass-produced publicity photo featuring three girls, clearly sisters. They were smiling big, happy, show-biz smiles and wearing black-and-white outfits and top hats. Two logos framed the girls, one in the bottom left and the other in the bottom right of the photo. The logo on the left was the symbol for the famous Cal Neva Lodge, a hotel, casino, and showroom that straddled the border of Nevada and California. The other label featured stylized script and said simply "The Gumm Sisters." Leland's eyes went from the bottom of the eight-by-ten to the top, just above the youngest performer's head, where he saw these words:

To Chester, Keep Smiling! Your Friend, Frances Gumm

It sent Leland's mind spinning back to his dream. His imagination produced a different type of time capsule, but one that contained oddly similar contents. The dream vault contained a mint-condition copy of the soundtrack to the movie *The Wizard of Oz*. The real-life reliquary had a publicity photo of and an autograph from Frances Gumm, who Leland knew later changed her name to Judy Garland.

There was a piece of art, far from professionally done, on top of a few other pieces of paper. The artwork appeared to be made with black marker and crayon drawn on a piece of heavy-stock sketchpad paper. Leland picked it up carefully, perhaps fearful that it would disintegrate from the pressure of his touch and his memories. He was looking at the face of a tiger whose left ear was partially hidden by some tall grass. He knew the drawing well. He had been the artist. First grade, he thought. Mrs. Cunningham, he recalled. The teacher had been so impressed by the six-year-old's talent that, in front of the class, she asked the suddenly beet-red Leland if she could display what she called his "Tiger in the Tall Grass" illustration on the elementary school's "wall of talent." The "wall" was simply a hallway, just off the school's main entrance, that led to first-, second-, and third-grade classrooms. She took Leland's embarrassed silence as permission. If he had, at the time, been able to find his voice, he would have declined the teacher's very generous offer. It did earn him an approving smile and wink from Katie Swanson, the classmate Leland considered the prettiest girl in the school, and an equally disapproving glare from his friend Scotty Sands, who fancied himself Katie's beau. It was exactly the kind of attention, even at six, he sought to avoid.

The last thing the adult Leland thought, as he set the illustration aside, was that he was positive he had never mentioned it or shown it to either of his parents. Yet here it was in a cardboard box full of memorabilia on the floor of his dead father's attic.

Pulling the long-lost piece of art from the box revealed several other sheets of paper, including certificates proving he was a very, very, very rich orphan. The combined sum of Leland David's wealth, much of it earned from his father's investments, staggered him when he first heard the figures. He closed his eyes and once again experienced the extravagance of the attorney's office. He felt so small amid all of the pomposity when he sat at the immense Peltogyne wood desk during the reading of the will. He found out it was Peltogyne because he asked, never having seen a purple wood table before. He never asked what he was suddenly worth; they just told him. To this day, whenever he took a moment to think about the money, it staggered him. He found it hard to concentrate on much after hearing the information, but he did manage to absorb what the bespectacled attorney said next. It might have been Leland's imagination, but he could have sworn the executor sounded envious as he read the words written by his father.

"I, Chester Daniel David, being of sound body and mind do bequeath all of my worldly possessions to my principal beneficiary, and only son, Leland David with the following two exceptions. First I leave the sum of five hundred thousand dollars to the Conner Suarez Project." Leland would have to find out what that particular charity, he assumed it was a charity, was. "Second," the attorney continued, "I leave the sum of one million dollars to Donald Richards." Lester was happy for both, would have been just as pleased, if not more so if his dad had left even more to each. It still left him with an ungodly amount of money and an old house. It was up to him to figure out what to do with both.

THOSE DAYS

"What a bunch of nincompoops!"

Emmett Lander looked up from his crossword puzzle and pulled the glasses away from his face. It was rare that he heard such an outburst from his wife.

"What happened, dear?" he asked, a little concerned and genuinely curious.

"Remember the big airport project my dad mentioned a while back?" She looked up from a letter she received in that day's mail.

"What happened, dear?" he asked again, as concern completely pushed out what was left of curiosity. "I was under the impression that particular enterprise was deemed unattractive."

"It was," she confirmed, "but apparently Gaetano's company had a different opinion." Lander knew Gaetano Lucchesse was better known by his nickname, Tommy. He also knew Tommy and his associates, especially one James "Jimmy the Gent" Burke, thought big but weren't particularly thoughtful. So, it didn't surprise him that the allure of millions of dollars in untraceable money would peak their interest. But Burke was a hothead. He had once even offered to fight Lander over the affections of the woman who currently sat less than thirty feet away.

"Seems there turned out to be more than five million dollars in cash," she said, shaking her head.

Lander whistled through his teeth. He recalled the specifics of the plan and remembered the number $2 million being bandied about. It was American currency from monetary exchanges made by US servicemen and tourists in West Germany. The delivery happened once a month, arriving on various airlines, and was temporarily stored in a New York airport vault. This time the money in question was stashed aboard a Lufthansa jumbo jet. The prevailing attitude among the group was that the risk, stout airport security, unsecure escape route, and other variables far outweighed the reward of two million bucks. Not to mention some of that money would have to be doled out to rival crime families as insurance. The group decided to take a pass. "I wonder if the decision would have been different if we had known the take was going to be five million and not two."

"Not to mention almost a million in jewelry the ninnyhammers decided to steal." Evelyn Lander went back to reading, or rereading, the letter.

"I'm guessing we wouldn't be discussing this if things had gone off without a hitch," Emmet said rhetorically. "How exactly did they screw the pooch?"

"Emmet, *please!*" his wife scolded. "Such language." She actually tsked her husband, and then smiled for the first time since her letter opener sliced through the top of the envelope.

"Sorry, my dear," the chastised husband muttered.

"Of course you're right," she added. "It seems those fellas forgot all about finesse. Went in full outlaw, guns loaded. Beat some people up."

"Sounds like the Gent" was all Lander said.

"Then somebody forgot to ditch the getaway van. Cops found it the very next day."

"Sweet Jesus," Lander exclaimed, "that's likely to get somebody killed.

"Already has," his wife responded, looking down at the letter again. "Stacks is dead." Lander knew the small-time crook they called Stacks. He knew he was pretty good at playing the blues and better at stealing credit cards. He was also trustworthy behind the wheel of a getaway car but apparently not all that proficient at getting rid of them.

"Something tells me Stacks is only the beginning."

"Daddy agrees." Evelyn Lander didn't look at Emmet as she replaced the letter in the envelope, pushed back from the table, and used the lit end of her husband's cigar to turn the information to ash.

THESE DAYS

There was one more piece of paper in the pile, and it was, without question, more confounding than the rest. The last proclamation in the box was actually a diploma of sorts, a recognition of achievement, a certificate of course completion from the "Jump for Joy School of Skydiving." He set it back in the box with the rest of the goodies and promised himself he'd revisit that part of his old man's past. There were a few more things in the box, and he turned his attention to them. He picked up a smooth, still relatively shiny piece of silver. Leland held it between the thumb and forefinger of his left hand. Instinctively he rubbed the metal. It was the size of a quarter, and Leland guessed that's exactly what it once must have been.

The last thing he found was actually three things, three magazines stacked on top of one another. He picked up the publication on top and noticed it was a vintage *LIFE* magazine with an artist rendering of a human head on the cover. Inside the head were three advent-calendar-like windows, open and revealing different images. Below them Leland saw and read the words, "The Brain Part IV, Chemistry of Madness." In smaller letters in the lower right-hand corner of the cover was a date: November 26, 1971.

He reached for the next magazine. It was an iconic yellow-bordered *National Geographic* with a smiling woman on the cover. She was holding a massive bouquet of orange flowers. The subjects written about inside were listed on the left side of the cover and included "Arizona's Suburbs of the Sun," "The Danube: River of Many Nations, Many Names," and "Comeback in the Caribbean—The Dominican Republic." At the top, above the name of the magazine, was the volume, 152, and the issue number, 4, on the left. The date, October 1977, was at the same level on the right.

The third periodical was a "Special Cruise Issue" of *Travel and Leisure*. The bow of a massive black-and-white ship graced the lower two-thirds of the varying shades of blue background. The top part, the part without the image of the vessel, featured *Travel & Leisure* in a peach-colored font. In between the ampersand and the *L* of Leisure were the words "February 1975" and "One Dollar." Leland had long ago realized his dad used the glossy weekly, monthly, and annual journals housed inside the attic as source material for his mostly fictional reviews of all the spots he "visited" for his best-selling travel anthologies. But why were these three magazines in this box and not the others?

Was there a clue in the covers? Was there a way to uncover the cover-up inside the pages between them? He thought again about the note his father's best friend scribbled out during the middle of a detailed dream. It was unreal how real it all felt. Twenty-two words in all, all lowercase, save for three. The second sentence read simply, "he was Doing the Best he Could." The letters *D*, *B*, and *C* in caps, the magazines, the skydiving certificate, the photograph, Leland couldn't shake the feeling that they were all connected, that it all meant something, but for the life of him, he couldn't figure out what.

"Potter, come," he called to the dog, completely oblivious to the fact that she was right behind him, flat on her back, sleeping. "Let's go home and pack." She was sleeping no longer. On the drive back to his house, Leland took the time to return Jeremy's call and via voice-mail accepted his invitation.

THOSE DAYS

Chester was on the road. He hadn't seen his old friend Don Richards in months, but that morning he woke up more refreshed, happy, and, in a word, complete than ever before. He was convinced that a trip, this trip, was necessary. Long ago his pal had indeed bought a cabin in the mountains, and then he won a bar in those same mountains thanks to a bet. He had also earned himself a nickname.

"They are calling me Snoshu," Don had said over the phone, "and I kinda like it." Chester remembered chuckling then, and he chuckled now.

"Congratulations," he told his oldest and, by far, best friend. "You finally have your nom de plume."

"Don't you mean nom de guerre?" Richards chided, and they both laughed.

It was a cast-your-fate-to-the-wind, clear-the-air, claim-back-your-life trip. He had given hundreds of thousands, if not millions, of dollars to various charities, funds, and organizations during his life that helped put a stop to beasts who preyed on kids like the kid he was. He made sure he would give hundreds of thousands more to a specific one the day he died. Whenever that day might come. But all of that giving, all the money in the world, couldn't conceal the fact that he had been, was still, a weakling. Afraid of the shadows in his past, unable to muster up the honesty needed to be a real father in the present to the son he truly loved. That was all going to change today.

It was a glorious day. A brilliant sun lit up an equally impressive cerulean sky. It had snowed a few days before and that blanket of white still covered much of the earth on both sides of highway, but the roads were clear, both lanes, both ways. The forecast for the next few days was devoid of more precipitation, and that was why Chester had decided to drive the Aston Martin. Lucille, with more condemnation than compliment, once called it his "James Bond car," and that made Chester love the machine even more. Richards had never seen it. The V8 Vantage alternately purred like a kitten and roared like a lion along the way.

"Lucille." Chester said her name with an oddly uncomfortable cocktail of sadness, longing, and regret. "Damn shame." He thought next of his mentor, friend, and father figure, Emmett Lander. He had made a boatload of money thanks to that old geezer. A great deal of it via illegal means and a good deal more, thanks to his own devices, through deceitful ones. There was also some legitimacy to his wealth, he thought wryly.

At his wedding reception, Lander "bought" Leland a celebratory cocktail and toasted the new groom with the same advice his father-in-law had given him on a similar night years before. "Buy life insurance," he said, before taking a sip. "Several million dollars of it for both your bride and yourself," he added after the drink. "Cuz you never know," he said, finishing the advice with a wink that momentarily made Chester uneasy. The new groom nodded and made a move to leave, but Lander grabbed his arm a little tighter. Chester turned and faced the old man who tried a smile but didn't let go. "I'm not sorry about the emeralds," he said bringing up a subject that still chaffed, "I did it for your own good." Chester took a second to process the words he didn't need to hear. He knew all along Lander didn't do it for him, he did it for Lander. He hadn't forgotten, never would, but he knew at some point he would stop caring. "I know," was all he said and this time he made a successful escape.

Later, at the very same party, Evelyn Lander found Chester and offered some interesting, more impressive words of wisdom. She suggested Chester take some of his money and invest in a relatively new New York three-letter company that specialized in the manufacture of business machinery, including commercial scales, industrial time recorders, meat and cheese slicers, and tabulators. The young man heeded the advice of both, and through a Lander family connection, of course, was able to funnel funds from one improper source into a couple of completely proper ones. On other occasions Mrs. Lander pointed Chester in the direction of other opportunities, namely, a different three-letter company, this one headquartered across the Golden Gate Bridge from San Francisco, hoping to make a splash in the movie business. Years before the wonderful woman had passed away, Lander, on his death bed, had the presence of mind to tell Chester to invest as much money as he could again.

"Apple," he croaked, not talking about the fruit. "My guys tell me it's a no-brainer."

He was smart enough to not ignore this dying declaration, and he didn't. He also wrote and published thousands of words telling people where to, and not to, eat, drink, visit, and be merry, and that ended up making himself, his wife, and his only child a more-than-comfortable living on its own. Through the years Chester David had taken a small fortune and transformed it into a rather sizable one.

He was a good provider to his wife of many years and his son of several years less. He knew this while also realizing he was a less than adequate husband and father. He didn't go to "career days" at his son's school, never encouraged father-son activities like Boy Scouts or YMCA Indian Guides, and, despite religiously contributing to churches, hospitals, and policemen's benevolent funds, he never attended any of the various groups' functions with his wife. He always had "work" and "travel" and "travel for work" as excuses, like the Thanksgiving he missed in 1971. Despite it all he was keenly aware that his little boy had grown into a fine young man. Healthy (he thought), happy (he hoped), and reasonably well adjusted for an incredibly rich kid (he knew). Unlike his old man, the boy (they had named him Leland) was extremely comfortable in his own skin and made friends easily. He was very good, not great, at a number of sports and at school. He was polite, personable, and even-tempered. He never drew attention to himself, which meant, to Chester's delight, he never drew attention to his father.

Chester crested the summit and began his descent. The sports car picked up speed. "I wish I could have shown you more love," he said softly, thinking about his son, not his former wife. *But I'm certain I loved you deeper and showed it more than my old man did me,* he thought but didn't say out loud. Leland was one of the things he always enjoyed speaking with Snoshu about, and he looked very much forward to seeing his dear friend again because this conversation would have a purpose. This visit wasn't going to be about convincing his old friend that coming clean was the right thing to do. It was simply passing along the message that after so many years, so many lies, it was the *only* thing to do. Fittingly, it struck Chester, Sinatra was singing *My Way* through the Aston Martin's custom Bang and Olufsen speakers. He reached for the knob and turned it up, way up.

The music was so loud that it made Chester question whether the sound he heard from outside the car was a blown tire (actually two), a gunshot, or his imagination. He took part of a split second to check for bullet holes in the windshield and another part of that same split second to realize he had lost control of the automobile, now careening wildly and crashing through the barrier between highway and mountainside, nearly seven thousand feet above sea level.

"Well, I'll be dipped in shit" were his final words as he unfastened the harness that held him in his seat, ensuring survival would be out of the question.

Should have taken the Wagoneer was his last conscious thought.

THESE DAYS

The sky wasn't quite as vivid, the road nowhere near as smooth, and Blue Canyon a less intense shade on this trip to the Sierra Nevada. But everything about the drive felt just as comforting in real life as it had in the life he led in the dream. He always loved making this trek. Along the way he tried to remember when and what he had eaten last. After only a minute or two, he came to the realization that it didn't matter; he was famished. So he took the exit for Colfax and found a McDonald's. Sitting in his car, in the parking lot, he gobbled up a Filet-O-Fish and a small bag of fries and washed it all down with a Diet Coke.

A few miles up and then down the road, he stopped again. This brief sojourn was due to the rumblings of the Berner and not his stomach. He knew she didn't need to put something *in* her body, quite the opposite. They were on the downhill side of the summit, enjoying the sunshine and the view. The pooch had peed, pooped, and pranced around, and now she lay near Leland's feet, head held high, eyes alert, left paw curled inward and underneath her furry white chest. For his part Leland had cleaned up after the dog and now sat, ass on the railing, head titled to the sky. His eyes were closed, but soaking in the sun through the lids, he could feel the heat and sense the reds, yellows, and oranges. He thought again about his dream and his dad.

Am I close to the spot? He wondered and thought he could be, but he wasn't about to inspect the barrier along the side of the interstate to find if this section was newer, more built up, safer than the rest. Had he taken the time, he would have discovered he was only a few feet away from where his life changed forever. He had seen the exact spot on television, along with the rest of the country. All the national network news broadcasts told the story of the well-known and respected travel critic who lost his life in a tragic, fiery, sensational car crash. It was all so surreal for Leland. He had just lost his father and he was hearing about it, along with millions of strangers, from Peter Jennings, Tom Brokaw, and Dan Rather. The latter's news report even went so far as to dispatch a reporter from the Reno affiliate less than an hour away to the scene. The other two just showed videotape that included skid marks, the battered barrier, and what was left of the Aston Martin, along with what it left behind as it tumbled down the mountainside. Perhaps the passage of time and his current state of mind made recognition impossible.

"Why didn't you drive the Jeep that day?" he said to the sky, eyes still shut, to a dead dad who he was certain couldn't hear him. "Time to go, Potter," he added, to the canine who he knew could. It was also time to find another eight-track to play on the rest of the way to his destination. He opened the case of cartridges sitting on the backseat and surveyed the selections. *I knew I got rid of all those Cat Stevens records.* He referenced his dream again as his fingers danced between the Eagles and the Sanford/Townsend Band. After some deliberation, he chose the duo. It had been a while since he'd heard "Smoke from a Distant Fire."

THOSE DAYS

"Is that everything?" The lawyer clicked the cap of his Waterman pen back into place and rested the top in the dent that helped define his upper lip. The frail old lady nodded her assent.

"Sorry, but you have to give me a verbal response," he said as he patted her tiny, wrinkled, yet incredibly perfect, childlike hand. She gently rubbed the fat part of his hand between the index finger and thumb—a spot that featured the small tattoo of a bear with a crooked spear running from its mouth to its tail. He remembered telling her it symbolized power, courage, and confidence. He also remembered her telling him she didn't care.

"Fuck you," Evelyn Lander half breathed, half grunted.

"I'll take that as a yes." He removed his hand from hers and put the papers back in his briefcase. Evelyn smiled.

"You're a good boy, Joseph," she wheezed.

"Thanks, Aunt Ev." He returned her smile and reclaimed her hand. "I'll make sure this is taken care of." The young man leaned in and kissed his aunt on the forehead before speaking again. "Can I ask you something?" He waited for either a nod or another fuck-you. After a second or two, he got the nod.

"I get most of this, and would never pretend to question what you want to do with your estate, but why would you leave your emeralds, this house, and the store to a stranger?"

Without hesitation and in a clear, calm voice, the old woman answered.

"He wasn't a stranger to us." She had a faraway look in her eyes. "And I know in my heart it's what Emiliano would have wanted."

The lawyer hadn't heard his uncle's given name in years but he had gotten his answer, and after another quick peck on the forehead, he stood, turned, and headed for the door.

"Joseph?" Hearing his name, he stopped and looked back over his left shoulder. "I'm ready to speak to a priest," she said, closing her eyes.

THESE DAYS

And like that jaybird flyin' home to Mobile
Girl, I'm campin' in your cornfield for a while.
Seems like I backed into a square deal
And I'm in for the night.

Leland sang along to John Townsend and Ed Sanford.
"I still can't believe these guys didn't make it big, girl." His eyes found the rearview mirror but couldn't find the dog, who clearly had no opinion. He lowered his eyes and saw the sign that informed him the exit for CA 89/267 was a mile ahead. He knew the three-digit highway would take him where he wanted to go. He ejected one eight-track cassette and popped in another. Ten seconds of simple guitar notes and drum beats burst out of his speakers.

"There's something happening here," sang Stephen Stills. "What it is ain't exactly clear." The dog's head appeared from behind the back bench seat.

"You like Buffalo Springfield, princess?" He smiled, his eyes back on the rearview mirror. As an answer the pup spun around slowly and resettled with a mild thud. She had heard the music from, and her master tell the story about, the midsixties supergroup made up of Stills, Neil Young, Richie Furay, Dewey Martin, and Bruce Palmer, who was later replaced by Jim Messina. He was sure he heard her let loose a sigh.

He took a right turn at the stop sign onto California Highway 267. The road passed beneath the wheels of the Wagoneer as it picked up speed, and Leland thought back to a group of friends, in somebody's garage, playing "Nowadays Clancy Can't Even Sing." He punched up track seven on the eight-track player and started singing the song he had sung so many years ago. He knew every word of the Neil Young track then, still did. He also knew if he had turned right onto Glenshire Road, it would eventually connect with Donner Pass Road and take him right into downtown Truckee. Leland was pretty sure Snoshu still owned a bar there but had no way of knowing if he was ever in it. Regardless, Truckee wasn't his destination this trip, so he continued heading along 267 as it became North Shore Road. The Jeffrey, Lodge Pole, and Ponderosa pine trees started to rise on the mountainside in his path.

> *Who should be sleepin' but is writin' this song*
> *Wishin' and hopin' he weren't so damned wrong.*
> *Who's sayin' baby, that don't mean a thing*
> *Cause nowadays Clancy can't even sing.*

He gave his past one last smile and then turned his attention to what the future might have in store. For reasons he couldn't explain, that made him smile too.

THOSE DAYS

D on Richards was where he almost always was since he found out his best friend wasn't coming to visit after all. On that unforgettable, fucked-up day, and before the man had left his home for the mountains, Don had spoken to Chester. Snoshu was thrilled at the prospect of the visit because far too many days had passed since the cohorts in crime had been together. But when his visitor failed to materialize in what he considered a reasonable amount of time, Don Richards began to worry. Actually, that was a lie. The feeling Richards experienced from his brain to his belly started well past worry, skipped over concern, and headed straight to distress. Chester David was never late. Don happened to have a police scanner in his basement, and he turned it on. It didn't take too long for Richards to realize his friend wasn't late this time either.

"I'll have another." He said the three words as the bartender was already refilling his glass with the Pappy Van Winkle.

"Just one more, Snoshu, OK?"

He nodded, knowing she honestly had his best interests at heart.

"You're a hard man to find," an unfamiliar voice said from behind him.

"Obviously not," Snoshu said without turning around. "You found me."

"Not without some effort," the male voice said, and then the man behind it came alongside Richards and plopped down on an adjacent barstool.

"Congratulations," Richards said sarcastically, raised his glass, and took a long pull.

"Why don't you buy me a glass of that bourbon?" the stranger asked.

"And exactly why would I want to do that?"

"Because my guess is what I have for you just might cheer you up." With that the man slid an envelope along the bar until it rested between Don Richards's elbows. For a moment Snoshu's eyes remained on the man's left hand and the small tattoo that adorned it. Then he turned his gaze to the envelope. It appeared official, and it made Richards finally look at the face of the man who delivered it. He was nice looking, clean shaven, and much younger than Snoshu. He also smiled a warm smile.

"I'm literally just the messenger," he said, grabbing the glass the bartender had just filled with the amber liquid.

Richards sat in front of a roaring fire. The delivery man had long since gone, and after a couple of "just one mores," a wobbly Snoshu had accepted a ride back to his mountain chalet. The correspondence remained unopened. He stared at the flames and wondered what message awaited him. Was it from Chester? If not him, who? He still found it hard to believe that his friend was gone. They both could have died a number of times, Richards remembered thinking more than once. One of them probably should have, Richards knew, after jumping out of a jetliner in the middle of a rainstorm. But this time Chester *did* die, blowing through a highway barrier and careening down the side of a mountain. Finally, Richards reached for the envelope and tore it open with a trembling hand. He read the words and laughed out loud. The guy was right, what was delivered had indeed cheered him up. He fell asleep on the couch in front of the fire, thinking about what was written in the letter and the contents of a safe deposit box.

The next day the new owner of a Reno house full of memories visited the bank, anxious to find out what other surprises awaited him. Alone in a small, windowless room, Don Richards found out. The box contained two items. The first was a book titled *D. B. Cooper: The Real McCoy*, written by someone named Bernie Rhodes. Snoshu picked up the hardcover publication and looked at a man, handcuffed and shackled, pictured on the cover. Richards had never seen the guy in his life. He opened the book and chuckled at the one word scribbled, in Emmett Lander's recognizable scrawl, on the first page: *Bullshitter* was all it said.

The other things in the safe deposit box made Richards smile as well: emeralds—some bigger than others, all round, brilliant, which Snoshu knew were worth a bundle. In that moment Richards realized Evelyn Lander had passed. A single tear formed and then trickled down his left cheek. She was righting a wrong, settling an old score, trying to fix something that had long been broken. Chester would never know but Snoshu would do his part, keep what he believed was rightly his and give the rest to another worthy owner. He had no idea what Leland would make of the gesture or do with the gems once they were in his hands. But he knew he would never sell his; in fact, he would never do anything but cherish it. Value both this treasure and the memory of his dear, departed friend. He closed the safe deposit box, put the Tucker Cross gemstone in his front right pocket, and got up to leave the bank. On the way out, he dropped the "bullshit" book in a trash can.

THESE DAYS

Leland drove up and then down, turned right and then left, along the all-too-familiar streets. Familiar, thanks to actual days spent here and there, but more recently because of the amazingly lucid, inexplicably detailed nighttime, lifetime worth of visions his subconscious brain cooked up while his conscious one slept. He slowed, occasionally hoping that a change in the car's pace would give rise to something akin to a confirmation that this wild-goose chase, disguised as a visit to his best friend, would actually lead somewhere. Another turn, no better luck. After looking right, then left, then right again, he turned left and found himself back on Lakeshore Boulevard. He drove west, knowing Jeremy's place was a little more than a mile away, just off Nevada Highway 431, the Mount Rose Highway. He came up on the fork in the road, and veering left would take him to see his buddy. For some reason he went straight, and Lakeshore became Tahoe Boulevard. He told himself he wasn't acting like a complete lunatic because he could make a left a little farther along on Village and still get to Jeremy's without having to turn around. He also told himself that he knew with every fiber of his brain and being that there was no such delicatessen called *Ahhh Capicola*, and there was never a pub named Catcher in the Rye. Not anywhere on this block, in this town, or at this place in time, but that didn't stop him for hoping, or looking, anyway.

To his right, on and off in view between the buildings and the trees, was magnificent Lake Tahoe. Fed primarily from snowpack delivered by the waters of the Truckee River, Leland had learned as a kid that Tahoe was the largest Alpine lake in North America and, by volume, the sixth largest lake in the country. One of his grade-school teachers liked to joke that "there were only five bigger, and they were all called *great*." The teacher always laughed; the kids, except the suck-ups, never did. Although Leland didn't laugh, he did think it was clever, and he never forgot it.

He continued to sneak a glimpse or two at the beautiful blue body of water and remembered, seemed to actually feel again, how penis-shrinking cold it always was. Instinctively he shivered. He turned his head to reconnect with the road and then looked left. A strip mall conspicuously flexed its modern muscles a few hundred yards ahead. The contrast between what was gorgeous on the right and garish on the left deflated Leland. *Maybe it's time to give this up,* he thought. Then he slammed on the breaks.

The dog banged into the back of the bench seat and scrambled to a standing position. She stared at the back of her master's head. Luckily for her, Leland, and the Wagoneer, the driver of the only car behind him, an old British racing-green Mini Cooper was alert and nimble enough to avoid slamming into the back of the Jeep. With a long, not very menacing honk, and a much more threatening extended middle finger, he was on his way. Leland couldn't care less, couldn't move, could barely catch his breath. He just sat there in the middle of the road and stared at the sign that had to be a sign. Just below NAIL SPA and above INCLINE INK TATOOS were the words MOBY DICK'S HOUSE OF KABOB AND BEER. There, in real life, was an establishment with a moniker that referenced a literary classic, staring him in the face, smacking him upside the head.

"You have got to be fucking kidding me" was what Leland said.

THOSE DAYS

In the days, weeks, and months since Chester David's death, Snoshu Richards struggled with the responsibility he felt toward his best friend's only son. He went back and forth in his mind believing he owed it to the boy to tell him everything, to feeling beyond positive that he owed it to Chester to tell the young man nothing. Sometimes it depended on the day, other times the night, and many times on how much he had had to drink. He found himself picking up the phone hundreds of times and putting it back in the cradle on an equal number of occasions. Every so often he actually got as far as nine numbers before hanging up. Mostly, though, he just held the phone in his hand, his fingers never touching a single button.

He'd watched Leland grow up, mostly from afar, thanks mainly to chitchat and snapshots. He was always invited to and felt welcome at family dinners, birthday parties, and holiday get-togethers, and many times he accepted the invitations. He liked Lucille OK, loved Chester, and grew very fond of being around the boy who became a man. He was accepted as part of the family but at the same time knew it was never, ever, his place to come clean to Leland about what he and his father had done. Death didn't change that.

On the one hand, every night he put his head on his pillow, pulled the covers up around his neck, and closed his eyes *without* having the confrontation, it felt like a small victory, a tiny relief. On the other hand, knowing the secret would still be there when he awakened dogged him like an ache that wouldn't be assuaged, a weight that never lightened. He couldn't, and now never would, be certain Chester carried the secret of their double life over the side of the mountain to his grave, but every chance he got he promised himself that *he* would. Every time he convinced himself that not telling the boy was the right thing to do, he was equally convinced that he would be unable to lie convincingly to the boy's face if the subject ever came up. And the subject was bound to come up. He had plenty of money stashed away in banks all across the globe and plenty of places he wanted to see. He knew there was one very big reason to disappear, couldn't think of a reason to stay.

He packed a bag, arranged for Cessna Citation II to be ready at the airport, and pulled out two envelopes and two sheets of paper. He wrote out a simple note, in all lower case letters, on one.

"here are the keys to my house. it belongs to you now. don't fuck it up."

He signed it "Snoshu," folded it, put it along with both sets of keys inside one envelope, and sealed it shut with a lick of his tongue. Then he set his sights on the second sheet of paper. He searched for the words before deciding he could sit there for the rest of his life and probably not come up with the right ones. So he wrote.

> Leebo,
> your father was a good man and my great friend. i
> miss him every day. i'm guessing you have questions,
> and my hope is, if you're looking for answers, you find
> them one day. sometimes those answers can be found
> in the things that are left behind.
> love,
> "uncle" don
> ps the car is parked at the tahoe truckee airport

Without another look, he slid the sheet of paper inside the envelope, but left this one unsealed. He wasn't quite ready to finish the task.

His plan was to put both envelopes in the cash register at the bar, then head to the airport, and be "in the wind" by the time anybody realized he was gone. He threw his bag in the backseat of the recently restored BMC Mini. Despite some fine work done by a top-notch mechanic in Colorado, it always took a couple of tries for the car to turn over. On this day, the little monster was being stubborner than usual, but the engine finally roared to life, and he backed out of the driveway. He rarely drove the quirky car, never much liked the way it handled, but he absolutely loved the irony owning a 1971 Cooper represented.

All the last-minute planning had made him thirsty, and he was dying for a Diet Coke. He knew he could get one at the oddly named fast-food restaurant just up the road, but he also knew the pretty, feisty blonde that owned the place would recognize him. Today, of all days, was one in which he didn't want to be recognized. He'd get a drink someplace else. Richards also let his mind wander to where he would go once he boarded the private jet. Then the brake lights on the SUV in front of him suddenly burned bright red. Richards reacted to the asshole slamming on his breaks in the middle of the street by responding in kind and averting disaster by inches. Pissed off, he leaned on the horn and then got even madder when the "bleat" that emanated from his tiny sports car didn't fully express his anger. Snoshu pulled around, rolled down the driver's side window, without looking gave the guy behind the wheel the finger, and sped off. Two blocks later, he mused that the offending vehicle looked a lot like Leland David's magnificent Jeep Wagoneer.

THESE DAYS

"I'll probably be right back, Potter." He cracked the back windows and exited the vehicle. He had spent a few more minutes blocking westbound traffic on Tahoe Boulevard before mustering up the courage to pull into the strip mall's parking lot. It only took another half hour of jumping through mental hoops—one marked yes, the other no, to get out of the car. Twice he decided he should turn around, but he never did, and as he reached for the establishment's door handle, he noticed his right hand was shaking slightly. *Get your shit together* he thought, and he took a long pull of the clean, crisp mountain air. *What do you think you'll find inside?* he wondered as he pulled open the door and entered. It didn't take long to find out.

There were a number of tables, the kind that are permanently affixed to the floor, some with two chairs, others with four, and a few with six. None of the chairs had legs; instead the seats were attached to curved poles that were connected to the tables. Each seat swiveled to let the consumer in and out. *Nice design* was his next thought, *eliminates screeching* and *theft*. A father and young son sat at one of the tables, and as Leland walked by, he heard the young man, mouth full of food, ask his dad a question.

"What do you get when you croth…"

"Don't speak with your mouth full of food, bud," the father interrupted.

"Oh yeah, OK, sthorry." The boy swallowed and then started again.

"What do you get when you croth"—he still spoke with an adorable lisp employed by most tooth-challenged children—"a vampire with a sthnowman?" The boy smiled broadly, exposing a mouth missing front teeth, knowing his dad wouldn't have the answer. Leland didn't either.

"I don't know." The father said what Leland was thinking. "What do you get when you cross a vampire with a snowman?"

The boy giggled, barely able to contain his enthusiasm. "Frothtbite!" he said, and laughed out loud.

"Good one," his dad said, rewarding the boy.

Good one, thought Leland.

There was space enough for at least a half dozen full-grown adults to line up in front of the counter that displayed three cash registers. Slightly above and directly behind the registers was an open rectangle, maybe four feet high by ten feet wide, that revealed a fast-food kitchen. If you looked higher than the window, you could see all the culinary delights that could fill your gullet at Moby Dick's House of Kebob and Beer. You could also calculate how much it would set you back. His eyes scanned the menu. As expected there was the Great White Whale, the Queequeg, the Melville, the Ishmael, the Pequod, and, of course, the Ahab. Leland had no reservations about whether this was a dream or not; he knew it wasn't. He hated Moby Dick.

There was no sound of a chime as he entered—no bell, no buzzer, and no one behind or in front of the counter. He looked at his watch. It was 3:20 p.m.—no surprise the restaurant was mostly empty.

"Hello?" he called out. Nothing. He waited another thirty seconds and called again, this time a little more loudly. "*Hello?*" Again no response. *Oh well,* he thought, more than a little disappointed, then he turned to head out.

"Be right there!" a disembodied female voice finally replied. Leland turned back around to face the counter. From a swinging side door, a girl, *the girl*, emerged.

"Hi," she said, drying her hand on a Moby Dick's, whale-tail shaped apron. "Sorry. Didn't know we had a customer." Leland stood stunned. This girl was striking. Beyond pretty, naturally beautiful, and the more he stared, the more he noticed she was no girl. He looked away because he had to blink and breath.

"No problem." He finally managed to stammer out a couple of words. "I'm not actually a customer." He added, still not looking at her.

"If you're selling something, we don't need it. If you want to put a flyer in the window, sorry but I can't let you do that. If you need to use the restroom, it's right over there."

He finally looked at her again and noticed she was pointing behind him and to his left. He took another deep breath and in it found a smidgen of courage.

"Not selling, no flyers, and I just went."

She smiled a slight smile, and his heart pounded.

"And you're not a customer," she said. He nodded. For the first time, he noticed a name sewn in big, navy-blue, cursive letters on the white apron: MAC. Leland smiled.

"Let me guess; your dad was a huge fan of Kesey," he said, a little smugly.

"Excuse me?" she answered suspiciously. Leland pointed.

"Your name—the name on the apron—it says Mac. I was guessing it's because your dad was a fan of the writer Ken Kesey and Randle McMurphy, the character in his classic *One Flew over the Cuckoo's Nest*. He couldn't name you Randle or Murphy, so he named you Mac." Finally, he finished babbling and flashed his most engaging smile.

"You're weird." Her smile was now gone. "And you're not even close." She turned away and headed toward the stand-alone fridge that held various bottles of beer, water, and soda. Undaunted, Leland pressed on.

"Well then what is your real name and how did you get it?"

Mac stopped, turned, and considered Leland. *He's nice looking*, she thought, *but a little strange. I'm intrigued, but who starts a conversation like that?*

"Why don't you ask him?" she said, turning her focus to a man back in the kitchen.

"Your dad's alive? Leland absentmindedly blurted out.

"Who the hell *are* you?" she not so absentmindedly blurted back. "And what kind of question is that?"

Leland was completely embarrassed but steadfast in his determination not to completely fuck what he perceived as an opportunity up. As he looked more closely, he noticed her hair was blonde, not brunette, and she wore it down, shoulder-length, not in a ponytail. He didn't know why he thought of that, but he did know he wanted to get the conversation on more solid ground. Wanted, no needed, to keep talking to Mac, to stay in her orbit. He asked the only question he could think of.

"Do you like dogs?"

She stared at him as if he had six eyes on two heads, but then Leland thought he noticed her eyes soften just ever so slightly.

"Doesn't everybody?" she offered as an answer, and then the smile was back.

Leland felt his knees go weak, but instead of falling on his face in Moby Dick's House of Kebob and Beer, he managed to smile back. "Care to meet mine?"

As it turned out, Mac's father had no idea who Ken Kesey was until Leland mentioned that he wrote *One Flew over the Cuckoo's Nest*. The guy said he really liked that movie, and Tommy Lee Jones was great in it. Leland didn't have the heart to correct him and tell him it was Jack Nicholson. Her dad revealed the impetus for his daughter's name wasn't one of the most famous *not* crazy, crazy characters in literary history. It was far simpler than that. Hank—his name turned out to be Hank—was army through and through, and General Douglas MacArthur was his hero.

Leland also discovered it was Mac who actually owned the restaurant—her dad worked for her—so she didn't have to ask for permission to leave. While she was preparing to do just that, Leland retrieved his phone from the front right pocket of his jeans and dialed Jeremy's number.

"I hope it's OK that I'm bringing a friend." He ended the message by ending the call. A few minutes later, they were still in the strip mall parking lot, sitting on the open tailgate of the Jeep Wagoneer.

"I'm really glad your parents didn't have a boy." Leland was on the left, Mac on the right, Harriet Potter in the middle. The dog looked at her master and then lay her head on the girl's lap. "I think she likes you."

"What's not to like?" She ran her hand from the dog's snout to the top of her head and then rubbed behind her left ear. Leland couldn't think of a thing. "Can I ask you something?" she added.

"Of course."

"Do you believe in fate?"

"You mean the principle that everything we do has already been predetermined? The concept that we have no choice, no say in the matter?"

"I mean, why did you come into my restaurant, smartass? You weren't even hungry."

Appropriately chastened, Leland thought for just a second. "I came to Tahoe looking for someone, and I guess I found *something* instead."

"My restaurant?"

"Your restaurant."

"Who were you looking for?"

"Doesn't matter."

"Maybe it does."

Leland stopped to think again and absentmindedly put the index finger of his left hand to his lips and started to gnaw on the nail.

"Don't bite your fingers."

"I'm not biting, I'm gnawing," Leland honestly believed there was a difference between the two, but he removed his finger from his mouth anyway. "I came this way looking for an old family friend, a guy named Don 'Snoshu' Richards. Heard of him?"

Mac said nothing. She looked for another moment at Leland and then turned to stare at the traffic passing by on Tahoe Boulevard.

"Told you it didn't matter," he muttered, and looked toward the street too.

"Let me ask again." Her right hand left the pup's head and found Leland's left. "Do you believe in fate?" Five words came out of the girl's mouth a second time. Potter yawned.

"No."

"Snoshu Richards owns a bar we go to all the time."

"Can I change my answer?" he asked.

"To what?"

"To 'I didn't use to.'"

THOSE DAYS

D on Richards looked at the calendar taped to the paneled wall beside the fridge. He had been on the island paradise for exactly a month and found himself liking it more and more each day. It was a calendar that featured quotes from famous authors. Above the days of this particular month was a picture of Frenchman Honore de Balzac, and in quotations one of his famous observations, "Laws are spider webs through which the big flies pass and the little ones get caught." He smiled.

Snoshu had everything he needed, made easier by the fact that he didn't need very much. Never had. He slid into his flip-flops and pulled on a mostly clean T-shirt. An advertisement for Abby's Highway 40 Cocktail Lounge was emblazoned on the front. Liquor, Poker, and Weddings were the offerings printed above the logo. He gave each armpit a quick sniff and headed out the door.

A few minutes later, he was sidling onto a stool and striking up a conversation with the woman behind the bar. She acknowledged his presence with a slight smile and a nod. It wasn't the first time he had been there, and on previous visits he had learned the bleached blonde wasn't merely the barkeep; she also happened to own the place.

"Hey, Babe." It wasn't a term of endearment. It was, he had also learned, her name. "Any idea how long it takes to get all the way around the island?" He had asked the same question in different ways before.

"Still no idea, but my guess is it can't be that hard to find out. Specially for a smart guy like you."

"Probably not." He paused. "Hey, did you happen to see the show about sharks on TV last night?"

"Worked here until two. TV was on, but folks were watching sports."

"Scary stuff," he said. "They talked to a surfer who had been attacked. Showed an actual shark tooth that came loose from the monster's mouth."

"Happens from time to time around here."

"Man. Really? Some so-called expert on the show said if confronted—that's the word he used, *confronted*—by a shark, you should try and punch it in the nose. Can you imagine!" Richards shook his head a little more dramatically than necessary and then added, "I would be scared shitless. But I gotta admit, having a shark tooth as a souvenir would be pretty cool."

"Are you gonna have a drink?"

"Sure, how about a beer?"

The bartender pulled a frosted mug from a cooler under the bar and filled it with liquid from one of the taps.

"Put it on your tab?" she asked, setting the beer in front of Don Richards.

"Please," he said, before sucking the foam off the top, "put it on my tab."

THESE DAYS

The Forty-Niner looked almost exactly like Leland remembered it, but he couldn't remember the last time he had set foot in the place. There were a handful of folks scattered around the room, none at the bar, where a woman stood sentry. Leland thought she was nice looking, for an older woman, probably a knockout not so many years before.

"Are you dog friendly?" he asked.

"Excuse me?"

"Are you a dog-friendly place? Do you allow dogs inside?"

"Look around, kid." She gestured with her right hand. "What do you think?"

"I'll go get the girl," Mac said, grabbing the key and heading back out the door. Leland took the remaining steps to the bar and pulled up a chair.

"What can I get you?"

"Actually, it's not a what, but a who."

"OK, I'll bite," she said. "*Who* can I get you?"

Mac walked the dog into the bar. The pup stopped and sniffed around a chair or two while the girl let out the leash and kept walking.

"Hey, Misty."

"Hey, Mac. Cute dog."

"Thanks. It's his."

"I'm looking for Snoshu Richards." Leland interrupted the reunion.

"Get in line." Misty shrugged. "Haven't seen him in more than a month, but it seems he stopped by recently."

"What do you mean?" Leland asked.

"The old coot left a couple envelopes in the cash register sometime between when I went home and when I came back."

Mac decided to take a shot in the dark. "This is Leland David. Was one of the envelopes for him?"

"It just so happens one was." Misty turned her back on the couple and opened the register. When she turned back around, she held a plain white envelope and a gun.

"Jesus Christ!" Leland cried, raising his hands.

"Whoa, Misty!" Mac barked.

Bark, Potter added.

"You don't have anything to worry about if you are who you say you are." The bartender kept her eyes on Leland. "But if you're not, you'll need something meaner than a Bernese mountain dog to protect you."

"He is!"

"I am! Let me get my ID out of my wallet." Leland's right hand went for his back pocket, while his eyes never left the barrel of the gun. "Here," he said, tossing the billfold on the bar, "see for yourself."

Misty did. Satisfied, she put the pistol back in its hiding place under the cash register and dropped the envelope in front of Leland.

"Sorry, Mac." She offered an apology to her friend but not to Leland. "Can't be too careful when that bastard Snoshu is involved." She walked away muttering, "Don't know why y'all got so worked up. Gun's not even loaded."

Leland looked at the envelope with his name written on the outside, taking a minute to calm his nerves. He noticed there was more than a piece of paper inside. With his hands still shaking slightly, he tore it open with the index finger of his left hand.

"Easy." Mac put her hand on his shoulder. "It's just you, me, and the pup." Leland took a deep breath. *And my uncle and maybe my dad,* he thought as he pulled out the note. He read it twice, thinking both times about the imaginary missive his "uncle" left him in his dream. The words were different, but he couldn't shake the feeling that the message was similar. He gave it to Mac. A number of things remained inside the envelope, and as he turned it over, they all tumbled out. Five bright green, round, gemstones settled in front of him. The sight took his breath away. Four were the same size, one was slightly larger. They all looked perfect.

"Are those real emeralds," said Mac, still holding the note, looking at Leland.

"My guess would be yes."

Another article that bounced on the bar was the key to a car. Leland recognized the logo and realized he was now in possession of Snoshu Thompson's Mini Cooper.

"Says here the car is at the airport."

"I'm sure it is." Leland got up, got a twenty from his wallet, and placed it on the bar. "Let's get out of here."

"What does it all mean?" Mac made sure the dog was in tow.

"Can I tell you a story?" Leland reached for the girl's hand.

"I guess." She reached back.

"It's a long one."

"OK."

Leland, Mac, and Potter got back in the Jeep and headed over to Jeremy's. After all he had told his friend they were coming, and he figured he'd take advantage of the opportunity to tell his tale just the one time.

THESE DAYS

Leland sat on the park bench, lost in thought, and absentmindedly rubbed the emerald between the thumb and forefinger of his right hand. The leash was in his left. Potter plopped down on the grass, alternately panting and sniffing the air. His heart was full, and the last vestige of a tear stubbornly remained on his cheek, waiting for a soft summer breeze to gently blow it dry.

He had just been on the phone with a woman from the New Jersey antibullying project for several satisfying moments. He expressed his desire to provide a recurring donation to the charitable enterprise, in his father's name. The representative on the other line couldn't contain her gratitude. She thanked him profusely and wanted him to know how many kids his generosity would help. The tears welled up in his eyes and his voice cracked when he told her he hoped that was the case. He added it was both something he and his father had wanted.

"Thank him for us," the woman said with pure joy in her voice, not knowing about or not remembering the gift previously bestowed by the David estate.

"I will," he replied, and then hung up.

The expected breeze blew, carrying the sweet scent of lilacs, licking the last of the moisture from his face.

"Ready to go home, Potter?"

The dog most definitely wasn't. Partly because she loved being in the park, mostly because she hated being stuffed into the tiny green car that her master, for some reason, insisted on driving these days.

"Mac's at home," he offered as incentive, hoping the dog would like the sound of it. She did.

Mac had actually been "at home" on and off for months. As he and the Berner wandered up the path toward the car, he thought about the whirlwind that had been his life lately. He did share his entire story with Mac, everything before the dream, the actual dream, and the crazy hours and days after the dream. He fretted, more than a little, that she was way too smart to stay after sitting through and sifting through the story of his life. The waking and nonwaking moments.

She not only stayed but also told him she thought it was one of the most interesting tales she had ever heard. She wanted in. She wanted to know more about his father, his mother, and his pretend uncle. And he let her in, *all* in. They spent days together going through the magazines and the memorabilia. They spent nights together talking about the implications, scheming about scenarios, trying to make sense of it, wondering how it all tied together. One night, in bed, Mac rolled over onto an elbow, leaned in, and kissed Leland full on the mouth for what he considered several wonderful seconds. Then she pulled back, ran a finger around his full, still wet lips, and said five words that roared in his brain.

"You should write a book."

And he had. They had. Using the periodicals and the prizes left behind as a roadmap, Leland demolished a life he *thought* he knew and reconstructed one he never imagined could exist.

"We're home," he called, after unlocking and cracking open the door. He had worried, worried still just a little, that the house would be empty when he came home. Another girl of his dreams—just that, a dream. He couldn't help it.

"In here," Mac answered.

Leland's heart bounced at the sound of her voice. He couldn't quite tell exactly where "here" was, but the dog headed straight for the voice, having no such trouble. It turned out "here" was his study. She sat at his desk, in front of his laptop, the glow from its screen adding just enough light to make her already lovely face divine. A few of his father's magazines were still scattered on his desk. They served as research, reading material, and material clues. The box of goodies from both his and his dad's past was in a corner, the latest edition of the *CDD Guides* on a bookshelf, the dog now at her feet. At that moment, and every moment since Mac came into his life, he knew he was the luckiest guy alive.

"I like it," she said, finally looking up and seeing him as if for the first time. "Why are you smiling?"

His answer came, after a few seconds and a handful of steps, in the form of a kiss.

"I like it too," he said, his eyes never leaving hers.

"I meant the book."

"I didn't," he said, lifting her out of his chair. He took her place then eased her onto his lap. It was a perfect fit. He smiled inside and out and then reached his arms around her waist and let his fingers find the keyboard.

"What are you doing?"

"Changing the beginning."

He found the opening page and placed the cursor at the end of the first six words.

My dad was D. B. Cooper.

He took her hand, gripping her index finger. She didn't resist. Working as one, they held down the backspace key and watched every letter disappear. He let go and went to work on his own. She watched as he pounded out what replaced them.

It was a dark and stormy night.

ACKNOWLEDGMENTS

First and foremost, my sincere and everlasting thanks go out to Jake Hirshland who enthusiastically accepted the job as the initial grammar and punctuation policeman on this project. He ended up doing so much more than that; offering encouragement and ideas that helped make this book what it is. As another father once said, with a smile, to his son…"You might have a future in this business."

Next a shout-out to Susan and Bob Green. They both agreed to read early versions, offer opinions, and check facts. Then they came back with corrections and suggestions that made the work better. To my friend and fellow writer Alan Winter who, after hours of coffee and conversation, said four words that meant the world to me: "You are a writer." And to the CreateSpace team who this time, like the last time, so expertly helped push this project over the finish line.

Most importantly I want to say thank you to my extraordinary wife, Sarah. You are both my inspiration and my rudder. But more than anything you are my dream girl. You make it possible for me to do what I love and I could not love you more.

While this book features events that actually happened, it is a work of fiction. The characters are figments of my imagination and any resemblance they may have to persons, living or dead, is purely coincidental.